MW00935889

THE LONG MORNING

and other stories

LEE LANDEY

The Long Morning and other stories
© 2020 Lee Landey and Chondritic Sound

ISBN: 9781546977506

Layout by Greh Holger.
Cover layout by Greh Holger & John Wiese.

Many thanks to all involved.

www.chondriticsound.com

CONTENTS

For Lin and Clayton, Dorothy, Max, Anne, Leon and all the Rest.

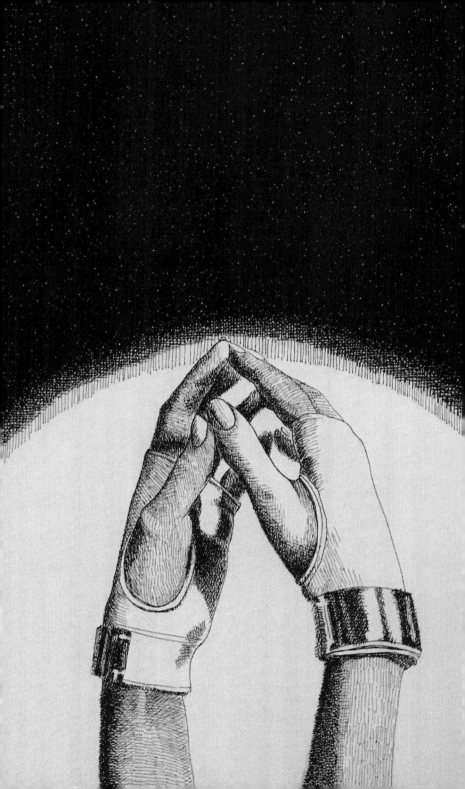

THE HOLY VOID

In the pitter-patter twilight of dawn I rose.

Or I rise, and have risen. The rose is of a gloaming I remember from long past, a rose on the horizon; petals of light shedding into dusk, over fields of cane, and a faint musk lingering above the rushes. Unwashed sweat, stale in a small hut by the reeds where I lay on a dirt floor beside my mother. She snored woefully. As now I rise upon stone, and later Biyu will snore next to me wrapped in fire-retardant mesh beside a corrugated bulkhead.

It is a slow rising, and a trickle of whispers rises with me. A murmur of flame at the end of an alley, where it banks out into a cobbled street; a face behind the flame, lambent above the rosy flicker. A murmur of mottled skin, translucent rings of fat bobbing atop a stinking marsh as we wade ahead, soaked through and fumbling. Freja in New York.

A pang shoots across the top of my eyes, arcing. My fingers rake across stone, and then I am sitting up, I am looking about. A cellar. I remember a cellar, yes. I recall contriving my way into a cellar.

Then, in childhood, and streaming sweat. I picked my way through red earth, scampered to a hilltop out from which I could see a neighboring village. Thatching lay raw in the sun, the image I have is of the sun, and it is so bright it grows fingers to feather across my lashes.

A hand above my eyes holds a shadow, and in the shade of a fever tree a crone handles a pestle.

There was a time in darkness, at Novyy Moskva, not long since the ganglers arrived, I sat with Biyu along a low aluminum bank where drinks were served through a slot in the wall. Biyu had on occasion enjoyed her drink, and we sat in the summer night as a drunk waltzed beside us beneath the pale green and vermillion shapes cast off the infinite heights of a banking presidium across the thoroughfare. He smiled at us through silver strings of spit, moaning some guttural thing caught at the top of his throat, a hum.

Biyu muttered a Cantonese slur toward him, a jovial "go away" that registered dimly in some quadrant of his face. He spread his arms wide, an upright moth against the ribald neon of the square, and began to sing:

> *I'll miss you in the morning*
> *I'll miss you in the night*
> *I'll miss you in the evening*
> *When the stars are not yet bright*
> *I'll miss you on the morrow*
> *When the gulls have had their fill*
> *I'll miss you in the morning*
> *You know I'll miss you still*

This will not happen for years more.

It has not happened, not yet, and I am moving west across the plains, for there is promise to the west. I move at night, as I always must move at night, and even were this not the case, who in these lands would care to look at me in favorable lighting? I am a specter of their carnage, I have raced apace their most horrific desires and arrived presently, scathed.

The crime and human mixture to the east was a true

revel, yet I departed with the opening of Erie, tired of the Irish. Freja and Oscar would stay for many years to come. The two of them could sink into any company, though their pallor, and not merely their disposition, could account for this.

Or it has happened? And I am crouched in a rocky maze, bereft of Biyu, out in the rings, and searching. There is a devil in the rings, uttering dictates to a seething army of slaves; a pale androgyne whose claws grapple at the black stony arms of a meteorite throne. Behind a brow sere and wan curl memories of a time when mountains were young. The devil sits unmoving, presiding over its morass of filth and greed.

In many years, greed has never abated.

How long is too long to sit in a cellar?
The light, hangs.

Out on the beleaguered front a craft from above soars down amidst crossfire, its shimmering apron of heat sizzling into the worn boulevards of contention. Biyu and I huddle for cover beside a munitions depot. The pilot leaps from the cockpit, unbuckling a cup of black rubber from his mouth; he reveals pale cheeks thrust forward from lines of grime sculpted by the mask's situation upon him, circling up from his ears, around, below his eyes, a child's drawing of an ellipse.

But then, on a Dutch ship I leaned against the prow, shifting my weight to the ornamented balustrade, my eyes straining into the distance. I was hungry, a deep hunger lined my veins and vessels with a thinness, a scraped-out-ness; I was in fact hungry the way that I am hungry now. In a cellar.

At that time I had yet to set foot in New York. Freja and Oscar were ahead of me, behind me too, but ahead of me. I was blind with hunger.

•

Waking in the mellow dust with the lights out.

Clambering about on rough stone. Sit upright, take a breath from habit.

A rose.

A yellow panel above buzzing alive with my movement casts piss-warm shadows across the hanging dust. A stone cellar. Voices descend as curtains.

Standing out in the fields, working, a heavy sun beating down. Coarse fingers around the splintered strands of a woven basket.

The roar, the haze.

I am standing in a street. Now, I am. The cellar behind me through a rusting shutter. The street is desolate. Dregs of neon worm through drooping displays along dilapidated storefronts. Radioactive fog creeps over building-tops, the stars a smear.

I walk through town, passing no one. I walk for miles, follow my nose, eventually sauntering upon a row of blacked out houses. I flit through a low gate; across the lawn whirring toys are scattered, clawing about the turf. The front door creaks open at a touch.

Within darkness looms. I stalk across the musty foyer, crinkled detritus strewn across the floor. The refrigerator door leans open, stinking of rot.

Down a creaking set of stairs to the basement, some moldering couches are angled together. Damp ash from a fire sits cold in the center, warm air wafting in through a smashed window at ground level. Some canned goods are tumbled about, nothing for me. How long have I slept?

I sit, wrap my jacket around me, lost in thought.

I remember, when last I lay down, bits of the city still sparkled and the low still walked the streets. A gurgle thrummed through neon haunts, and we danced through the radiation. The din of commerce capered beneath flashing green lights, towering faces lit every glass edifice, a glowing visage of fear – that nexus of human caprice and the imperium of capital.

Most had emigrated, but the remnants of civility lingered on. Violence took on a passion and a glamor, there was a lawless whimsy to everything. Even so, I was tired. The new breed of sociability was perhaps more inclined to accept my likeness, yet still, they took to me as caricature, and it rang untrue. My scars perhaps seemed romantic in the pounding blue of the nightclub, but after centuries I was scarcely less weary of their kind just because they now found me fanciful.

When I would take them into the back rooms, in the blinking moments, in shadow, in cushioned dusk, I would taste their salt before their iron, and I would show them a fervor, an intent, and a purity that the dispassionate relations of history had erased from the Earth.

Perhaps they have all left, or died off.

And what of my kind? Who is to say? If I'm all that is left am I, then, the authority?

Standing, I move to the shattered window and look up past blades of artificial grass; back through the murk to the few stars visible, made quiet by the fog. Have they all passed beyond?

I move out of the house down sweeping roads, pale and fissureless. I walk for miles, hungry. Eventually I come to barren rock, red waste, heaps of refuse and buzzing dust, crackling with cancer. Moving through the reaching crags of charred limestone, I climb down into dry gullies and cracked ravines.

Coming finally over a low rise I see one of the old scavengers hovering, moving from junk pile to junk pile. Its hull glints dully in the irradiated half-light, turbines humming softly through the haze, mechanical arms sifting.

Hollow sweeper lights affixed to the belly's casing rove over the terrain scanning for mineral deposits.

Cautiously I move forward. Manned or unmanned? Can't see through the tinted fore-shield, though a glimmer of crawling vector data glows through. It looks equipped for extra-atmospheric travel. Perhaps manned.

Silently I run across the rock, my jacket billowing behind me, and I leap, arcing up through the air, skidding across the top of the craft. It jilts downward with my landing, its search coming to an abrupt halt. One of the mechanical arms rakes up out of the flotsam to grapple blindly at its topside, its pincers whipping toward my face. Wrapping my hands around the shaft, I rip it from its trappings with a crunch and toss it down into the junk.

Skittering forward like a spider, I smash through the tinted visor. The drifting vector readouts turn to liquid around my fist, revealing a grimy figure huddled in the cockpit, sweating through the rags of his syndicate coveralls, scrabbling frantically back as the black glass rains down into him. I swing down into the cockpit, clawing towards him as the thrusters stutter and the craft falls with a crunch into the trash-heap.

The green spittle of Venusian rainleaf leaks out his fear-pursed lips to mingle with his sweat as I curl forward, and as his eyes drift over my face I see the look that I have seen a hundred thousand times: fear and disgust, mixed with wonder. My canines push down painfully from my palate, there is a great stirring within me, and I think of the fields as I take to his throat, a thatched hut, the work in the sun. For the first time in ages I chance to remember my mother's face. I feel now that, while alone, I have no owner, there is an openness to that, and drifting through the hot fields, alive with song, I love the man beneath me until I am no longer hungry and he is dead.

•

In darkness I persist through trash and stone, taking shelter in lifeless caves and leaning ruins when the sky begins to lighten. I find an old highway and stay with it for several nights more until I can make out a craggy lip of metropolis on the horizon; sallow faces lurch and lilt across the toothy wreckage, stammering along the skyline.

Passing through the outlying suburbs I enter a track housing unit to sleep one more cycle as it starts to get light.

I make my way through wide, creeping streets after dusk has settled, the sky glowing faintly above. Winding about in a desperate circuit, the city feels a vertiginous maze – each stilted high-rise trod across by the vestige of some stumbling countenance, pixels misfiring, degraded audio artifacted in echoes. Half-thoughts and the crescents of syllables ring down through the city grid: a sliver of war, an elision, a stutter of skincare.

This is where the others last retired, but how distant a memory is that?

I drift through abandoned groceries, shelves picked clean, upended barcode lasers dancing along the ceiling. Back out into the derelict streets, hovercars stilted like dominos down the curbsides, I amble my way in darkness to the central bank.

Passing through the empty frames of automatic doors across the dust of their convulsed glass, through rows of cubicles, I move up and over the aluminum teller barrier; inforeads lie cracked and broken, shattered tablets, shards of milky glass sprinkled like Pez.

Down marble steps, the soles of my boots clack against the brass rimming. The vault door has long been left ajar. Within, a yawning horseshoe of safety deposit boxes is ransacked, the walls a titanium honeycomb. Across the floor scattered jewels and necklaces are littered, coins and bills, documents of multi-federal citizenship and syndicate holdings, remnants of the last days of paper. Pearls skitter across the floor like marbles as I move across the room, clattering into the walls.

I approach box 1703D, still closed, and wrench it apart. Reaching inside I grope to the back until I feel the cool touch of recessed metal beneath my fingers, and push in. With a click, then a reluctant groan, a portion of the bank of deposit boxes shifts back into the wall and grumbles away, revealing a successive marble staircase leading farther down.

LED lights blink to life as I descend, lining the ceiling and walls. Confronted with a final burnished portal I thrust it open, only to find – nothing.

They have all gone.

The living quarters remain mostly intact, though the blood tanks have been drained, their nozzles dangling limply in the dust.

At this final absence I must wonder: am I the last or have we followed them? Have we finally rediscovered – what is it that we have lost for so long, our intrepidity? our imprudence? our childlike adventure! – and taken to the stars?

I notice along the wall a long metal cylinder sits closed like an iron lung. I move across the chamber to it, brushing away the grime. Flickering readouts dance across its surface, spitting garbled old runic morphemes, indicative of thralldom, blood slavery.

My fingers find their way to the release knobs, and with a sharp hiss of decompression the canister cracks open, the lid folding gently back.

Inside lies a young girl; pallid, a knee curled to her chest, eyes closed, lips apart. A small brand of ownership in the cleft of her throat. Her matted hair clings damply to her face. I stare. Left behind in slumber; much like myself.

I press my wrist to her open lips and, still comatose, she reflexively bites down, drinking until her eyes open, her muscles remembering. Slowly she sits up, mute. Her eyes brush over me, the empty slats, the drained tanks, the flickering displays dancing across veined marble. I help her out from her fetid sleep chamber and we make our way together up the stairs.

Back through the streets ancient ads still skip and falter, a juddering cacophony. The blind haze of radiation hums about our heads. Her figure is small beside mine, she cups an arm around my waist, dragging at my jacket for support. Beneath heavy lids a deliberate gaze sweeps to and fro, curbside to curbside; curves up then, parabolic, to move from my chin to my nose, my eyes, then past into the choking dust and faint green death that hangs above. Her eyes move, aquiline, as though counterweighted by a vein of rope to her heart.

The scavenger out in the wastes was no bother, I figure. My mind wanders back to that craggy abyss, dotted by the meandering hulks of syndicate drones. Extra-atmospheric, I would say. Certainly. I look up through the haze, the girl hobbling along at my side, up toward space, toward whirling dust and reaching infinity; toward food.

PRESENCE

It happened sometime in spring. It was still cold outside and there was a moisture in the air, the sky shot through with huge clouds scooping and ducking and then sometimes frozen with a cold fire. It was before the drop, when everything came crashing down, and the waves fell, when the bridge collapsed and I could taste salt and I watched the tilted thrust and rosy pulse as everything was crushed beneath.

It was very calm the day it happened, I was working in the city at the time, she was attending university. We lived together in a small flat above a corner store, rent-controlled, as it were, so we had gotten lucky in that way. We both had the day free and so the decision had been, if I recall, to hop in my jalopy, famed now between the two of us, and drive off to the country for the afteroon because to hell with the rest of them. The city had become cloying in that way that it does, climbing like steam pressure until one feels much as a rambling locomotive; and so these bi- or triannual drives to the country were something of a necessity for us.

The basket was packed, sitting in the backseat with a folded blanket brought for guarding against the dew. A fresh pack of cigarettes was tucked into the front pocket of my shirt, she was wearing a favorite skirt of hers which she had pulled up over her hips in the sleepy aftermath of a brief morning tussle, and her hand lay in my lap as the jalopy

19

whipped around broad curves skirting the uneven edges of green hills. We were ready, or so we thought; duly prepared for the rigors of a slothful afternoon.

When she disappeared I remember thinking nothing of it for a time, and I continued to nibble idly at what was left of our afternoon stores, flipping through a novel I'd been meaning to get to. I remember hearing a strange whirring. When she didn't return, I began to search, at first out in the wide fields, trying to make out her shape in the tall grass. When this proved fruitless I wandered in past the tree line, coursing around rotted trunks, scattering brambles in my wake and growing more frantic by the hour. Eventually I became unsure of myself, realizing that I couldn't recall the exact moment she had left.

Running through the trees, my feet crunching through the moist bed of shed foliage, the air was filled with the sharp scent of fresh pine. Eventually it began to darken, and with no flashlight I soon became lost.

The nighttime sounds of the woods swelled around me, and I continued to wander through the trees, not knowing from which way I had come. As I fought my way forward, batting branches from my face, I thought I saw a small clearing ahead of me. I remember as I approached it the sounds of the woods began to fade, settling to a muffled haze that lay somewhere behind and about me. In the faint glow emanating from the break in the pines, I saw that before me stood a figure. Drenched in dimness I could make out no details but its shape, which was man-like, but somehow stretched and looming, or insubstantial, its skinny shoulders bowing above me. Slowly it turned and in the blackness that was its face I knew it looked to me, and it told me – in no language – to leave.

Turning around I ran desperately, not knowing where I headed, my heart stamping painfully against my ribs. After an indeterminate time I finally broke through the tree line to find myself back at the highway, my breathing ragged. In the moonlight I could see the shape of the jalopy a ways down along the roadside, and I continued toward it as best I could. Finally, jumping in, I turned the car back towards the city and drove.

She was gone for a week. I called out of work, saying there was a death in the family. I found it excruciatingly difficult to fumble my way out of bed. There was a harsh fever upon me, and I consumed nothing but water for days.

Finally, one night there was a banging at the door. I shuddered forth from a black sleep and looked to check the time, but the clock was blinking midnight as though a surge had reset the power. I stumbled out of bed and limped through the sitting room to the front door. Peering through the peephole I could see nothing but darkness. Slowly, I pushed it open.

There was nothing there. Confused, but exhausted, I turned to head back to the bedroom and was startled terribly to see her shape standing there in the darkness. I stumbled toward her and she took me into her arms, placing my head against her breast whispering "Shh, shh, shh," all along.

Together we fell into bed.

In the morning I felt alive again; but there was something different about her, something changed. She knew it as well, and understood also that it was apparent to me, but felt as though it wasn't something which required discourse. It was just the way things were now, and the way that they would be.

There was an electricity to her, and I intimate this not as romantic hyperbole; she had a charged aura. Her hair would begin to lift as though in the presence of static, and when she would touch me it would send an unpleasant jolt through my extremities, and send my heart racing.

In the months before catastrophe, we grew closer in

some ways and more distant in others. Physically we grew apart, but it was as though she needed me to understand her change. She needed it as a form of grounding before she could act; to consummate her great work of rote and blue fruit. And when her change would become apparent, when it would manifest in various ways, it was to be nothing but understood. For instance, when she would turn on the television with a glance.

This, in a way, was the strangest of all: that her strangeness to me became eventually implicit, as though she had always been this way. In the time before disaster struck, it was as though the electricity that she had represented to me within had become a part of her; but because I had already felt it, the external mode of its manifestation came somehow as no revelation. It was a natural extension of her presence.

One night I heard her running a bath and I walked to the bathroom to be with her. I found her naked on the tile, against the wall, her hands thrust forward. The heels of her palms met, with her fingers stretching wide, and the water that ran from the bath's faucet snaked through the air towards her. And where it approached her palms, it cascaded away in shimmering waves like the plume of some magnificent translucent beast.

I knew we were almost there.

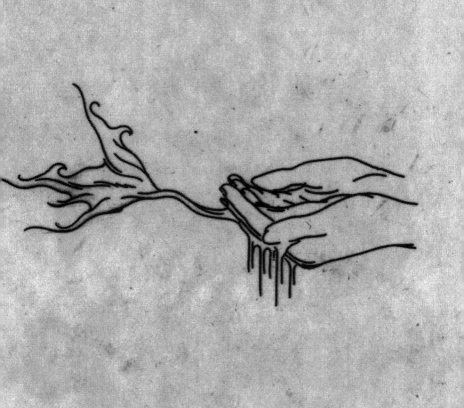

THE REPLICA

It is 0237 SST out in the folds between worlds, we drift around stars and I look to Biyu. Biyu makes a sculpture of old yogurt containers, a blue curving thing that is bodily, and coated in clinging tendrils of coagulated dairy. Starlight plays across its dimpled surface and the panels of the cockpit.

"Tell me again," says Biyu.

"Which one?" I ask.

"The one where Freja takes you to the fair. The White City." I clear my throat, and stare out to a million twinkling suns.

"Again?"

"Again."

"I was back in New York," I say. Biyu nods, dabbing at the yogurt across blue curves. "My mission west was a wash." Biyu snorts.

"A catastrophe," she says.

"I was young."

"Older than me."

"Biyu, would you like to hear about the fair?" She smiles and wipes a smear of yogurt down the plastic of her jacket, saying nothing, intent on her work. "I was back in New York with Freja. Oscar was on a tear."

"One of his tears," says Biyu. I swallow.

"He was furious. There were rumblings that they were to build an underground transit system in the city, we didn't have that yet, you see. Plans wouldn't be formalized until the following year. It wouldn't be finished, in fact, until a later fair, in 1904. But rumblings all across town, they were to rip it all up, the streets, the sewers, it would all be rubble; such was the bavardage.

"Oscar and his friends had a great deal of real estate beneath the streets and they were all in a tizzy, would they be discovered, where were they to move, etc., etc. Freja was rather tired of the ruckus; when Oscar was on a jag he was quite a creature. She figured the boys would sort it out at any rate, and back then I was often in agreement with however Freja was feeling. My trial separation from the Danes had not sat well with me. I would eagerly follow the flow of her hair, the way it would glance off a pale shoulder, whichever way it led me.

"And *Freja*... she wanted to go to the fair. There were other rumblings, you see, or headlines rather, great broad ones for many months of the Exposition that was to take place in Chicago. It had been 400 years since Christopher Columbus had set his cursed feet on the sandy shores of the New World — and 424 years since I was born, mind you — and the white world had a mind to celebrate.

"They built a great false city."

"The White City," says Biyu.

"The White City." She tears a strip of robin's egg container and compresses it to an adjoining edge with a squelching flourish, a squirt of yogurt ebbing from the newfound crevice. "There were to be attractions from the world over. A ceremony of unmatched gilding, of fuss, symbolism and portent so fastidious and grand it was to be beyond discounting. For two such as ourselves, awash in the tides of history and clinging madly to the bulwark of memory, fumbling as children for the surety of the Record, the unshakable Chronicle of the celebrant, it was an occasion not to be missed.

"Following a lengthy train ride along which Freja and I

curtained our compartment and spent a warm span beneath bedsheets," Biyu, covered in yogurt, rolls her eyes, "we found ourselves along the protracted banks of the great water pool, an ode to Christo's long journey and a silent shrugging-off of that same stretch to be trekked by dark millions below decks in the centuries that followed.

"Freja, while sympathetic to the plight of my distant past, was still inclined to find some marvel in the artifice of enterprise, and in moments such as these wanted to allow herself that rare sensation of wonder. Her ancient and pale heritage had imparted to her that tired disposition of reverence toward the grandiose, the more meticulous the construction the more sacred the observance. She liked great sweeping things. I wonder at our connection on occasion. It seemed she often found my greatest convictions to be rather trifles yet worth humoring. And still for a dizzying time I continued to humor *her*.

"I found her knowledge of our history to be of endless comfort. She taught me my English, and I believe I still lean upon the vestigial patterns of speech she then instilled in me. In many ways she taught me how to be. When the Danes first happened upon me my thirst was veiled pathetically behind a flagging *lançado* veneer. She dredged me up from that mongrel state, a village boy turned to that blood-covered thing. I am, in some sense, her colony.

"For so many years I found Freja to be my guide, and Oscar, though at times we have been known to thrill one another, an unavoidable component of that equation. Freja was the soft and humming light that bore me through the night. And yet this loyalty of mine circumnavigated her apparent estimation of me. Perhaps this speaks more, then, to my own assessment of my worth at the time.

"And so in Chicago on the crystalline banks of the Grand Basin, an ersatz Atlantic, we wandered the pallid symmetries of this artists' city, a blueprint of a thing that was, despite my dour ruminations, in a word, marvelous!

"We traipsed across canals, ventured 'round the sparkling lagoon and beamed up at the pearly façades, headquarters for Agriculture, Horticulture, Transportation, Machinery, Anthropology, on and on into the hazy future. And everywhere, even in the dimmer hours of operation that we have made our province, endless citizenry flocked across the avenues. We waded through whirling knots of visitors, a phantasmagoria of American flesh.

"Many of the exhibits closed early for the evening, but the streets were alive with a massacre of festivities. The scent of fried dough punctured the vacuous lakeside chill, and sweet Freja held my hand with both of hers, tugging down as we ambled, a contented child rejoicing in the folds of another.

"Beneath the thundering revolutions of the first Ferris Wheel I kissed the space between her eyebrows, each of her eyelids, and paused at her mouth to tell her that her head lay upon the pillow of my rakish heart. We soon found ourselves in one of 36 clanking cars rocking atop that vast contraption. Light pollution was then not as it later came to be, and vaulted up to the spangled stratosphere the sky was of nauseating delight. From the freezing pinnacle we could see the hairline branches of the terminal railroad threading into the fairgrounds, the glittering top of the Administration Building leering over the long Basin, the black sheet of Lake Michigan stretching out beyond and disappearing into a pall of stars.

"On our descent, as we looked out over the harbor we could make out the masts of three great replicas, the *Niña*, the *Pinta*, and the *Santa Maria*, bobbing at their moorings. The sight imbued me with icy hilarity, and once back on solid ground we pushed our way into the mutinous crowds and fought through to the brink of the wharf.

"We climbed aboard the *Santa Maria*, and I spent a quiet age roaming the deck of that unseemly facsimile. Columbus had lived a while on Madeira, the old epicenter of my hardship. He had married the daughter of a local governor on Porto Santo, an island in our archipelago, and they had settled there for a time. This was before his later deeds of note, and a fact I became aware of only subsequently. In every practical sense I have no connection to the man, nor would I care to. Yet this grotesque tribute of form, it felt as a lever thrust up from my home. In walking across the creaking boards of this idiot venture, waltzing sickened along the gunwale, it was the first instance I felt truly unhooked from the wheel of time.

"Here was that sought-after Record, that definite Thing made horribly real in the whorled oak of 19th century America; all the certainty the two of us craved now bearing form in this maelstrom dreamland of mechanical amusements and Grover Cleveland.

"I am told that at the Exhibition's closing ceremony the *Santa Maria* and her sisters cast off from the wharf and dropped anchor some several hundred yards off the shore. They lowered small skiffs, as if just arriving, and a thespian Columbus posed at the prow and took a land-ho stance with sword and flag in hand, urging the endeavor onward. The farce continued in exquisite measure as play-actors pantomimed monks kneeling in prayer at the beach, natives parading out from Bahamian foliage to greet the landing party. And so there in Chicago in 1893 on the edge of Lake Michigan, the simulacrum was consecrated in a display of buffoonery, and Christo's terrible exploit was made both holy, and unreal. And in my and Freja's search for a bastion of surety, we found instead the unmaking of time.

"In the years that followed, the ships fell into disrepair. They hung there at the jetty unused, carrion for vandals, stripped and robbed of wealth and meaning, languishing in the harbor. In 1911, at a later degraded ceremony, they were dragged back out from their moorings and tasked with another jaunt up the coast, a hundred thousand faux Indians hooting and jabbering along the beach as the ships made

29

their way north toward what later would become Millennium Park. Yet before the pageant could reach its completion the *Santa Maria* was forced to turn back for port, her crew and actors aboard worked into a frenzy as the hold began to take on water.

"In 1913 it was decided, in a spirit of dubious optimism, that the three rotted hulks would sail to San Francisco to retire. This was to involve a radical procedure wherein they would sail down the drainage canal into the Mississippi, onward to the Gulf of Mexico and through the Panama Canal to finally land at that California bay. The routing was upended several times and reports from hereafter vary, but from what I have made out the *Niña* and the *Pinta* made it as far as Buffalo when the venture's sponsor found himself bankrupt and abandoned the proceedings. The *Santa Maria* stubbornly kept on to Rhode Island where she was finally grounded and judged unfit to sail. She was later purchased for $940 at an Admiralty Court auction and was towed, alone, back to Chicago. In 1918 the *Pinta* sank. In 1919 the *Niña* burned.

"The *Santa Maria*, settled listlessly at the site of her heyday, endured further halfhearted restorations and expiations and persisted until 1952 when she was demolished by crane in a final act of municipal ambivalence.

"The White City itself, façades darkened by pollution in the months that followed the Exposition, caught fire in January of 1894. The blaze, attributed to tramps, began in the Casino before meandering through the Peristyle and on to the Music Hall. Showers of sparks fell to the ice-covered lagoon, enkindling a sea of fire – to the bedazzlement of spectators – that raged into the streaky daybreak as a stiff southeasterly wind carried the flames through the rest of the City. It is perhaps the wicked vagrants, if indeed they were here at fault, who must burden themselves with the mantle of hero.

"To belabor the point: in 1998, in mad obstinacy, another

replica of the *Santa Maria* was built at Madeira, my old home. Tenacious necromancers dredged her tired memory, gasping from the gills of purgatory, once more onto the blinding shore of the real to bask in balmy winds beside the sugar cane and laurel. To what end that final model sailed I do not know.

"At the prow of the ship that night Freja wrapped her arms about me from behind, and wailing, I retched blood into the water.

"The thing that we wanted was sanctuary; some acknowledgment that in living, and dying to yet still live, we were not mad. The anchor of our ancestry was instead contorted to skew us by a youth so implacable it too was ageless. We never found the dawn."

Biyu nods resolutely as I come to silence. I look up as she plasters yogurt down the final seam of conjoined plastic, rotating the structure to face me. Starlight plays in her eyes through the viewing shield as I come to see that she has stuck together a baby blue reproduction of the *Santa Maria*, plastic sails flared out to catch the solar winds radiating through the void, and I reach out a hand, in awe, to touch this further copy.

THE NEWS FROM NEW YORK

The news from New York was that Roman Pollard had pulled his support from Heaven Forbid.

Playing over every surface, his limbs skimming across the burnished steel of each desk in our office, he stood on the broad steps of the Hackney Building in midtown Manhattan, the dull morning sun playing off his hairpiece as he drawled, his eyes fixed just above the camera:

"I do, howsoever, regret to inform my constituents of my withdrawal from what once was our guiding light of reprieve, the true beating heart of American hope, now a stifling miasma of partisan venom: the Heaven Forbid Act, drawn up earlier this year by Dartmouth & Green. While it has long been my belief that our brave and holy force of Police deserve most especially that equipment and know-how necessary to scorch our streets clean of menace, that growing force of Evil which desires nothing but the reckoning of our dignified American society – though I truly want nothing greater than to see our enemies boiled back to the vileness of the increate – it has, to my great dismay, been brought vividly to my attention that Dartmouth & Green's Heaven Forbid would require too great a taxation on the American people, and that until we can find a more efficient and *bene*ficent way to pay for such an undertaking, it would be ill-advised to impose such a burden on the precious Joe and the precious Jane in the dear communities of our heartland. Let the Big Man Pay! That's What I Say."

He cleared his throat and tugged on the hem of his blazer, his lapels flattening across his wide chest in the heat. At my desk I increased the brightness and opacity of his image so that I could no longer see the gleam of my bureau through the doughy creases in Pollard's brow.

"These years since Arrival have been trying, and the criminal element crawling beneath our Great Society has certainly profited in unspeakable ways from the technology left behind by those foul immigrants from above. I recognize the argument, and I *approve* of the argument. Let me not be misunderstood! Our Police do indeed require the new weaponry deployed by the thieves and gangsters who ransack and terrorize our Singular Nation if they are to effectively combat them. There is no sense in prolonging the ban on official use of alien tech. My stance on this matter remains unwaveringly intact. But Heaven Forbid is not the answer! Not for us. Not for me. Not for you. We cannot put the charge of that effort to the Common Man. Trust me, America: There is a Better Way! That's What I Say."

Pollard gripped the lectern with both hands before raising them in curled fists above his head, his palms facing the swaying crowd that drizzled him with polite applause.

As he stepped aside, smiling, he was replaced by The Big Fat Idiot in his usual garb of startling colors and flowing gauze, blundering about the stage and guffawing, painted whiteface running down his cheeks. Turning his backside to the crowd of reporters he let out a tremendous fart as they cheered, and Pollard stepped back into frame to give him a wild smack upside the head, holding aloft his sticky wet palm to the cameras as The Big Fat Idiot reeled away, howling in mock agony.

Around my cubicle the murmurs began, as the scene at

the Hackney building faded back to the newsroom where an anchor fiddled attentively with her papers across a plexiglass workstation. I flipped off the viewing panel at my desk and stood up, heels of my palms against my eyes.

"Sue!" someone called, and I looked up to see Ivan Mural bounding across the microfiber carpeting, past the windowed boundary of the directors' offices, to the wall of my cubicle. Reaching my desk he put a hand over the barrier, leaning. "Sue," he said again, "did you see?" He was panting lightly, his speech breathy.

"Everybody saw."

"Evanston nearly had a heart attack." Mural shook his head, looking around us. "Was almost worth a laugh if it weren't such shit news for quarterly bonuses."

"It doesn't make any sense."

"You'd think the one thing you can count on is bastards being bastards."

"Yeah," I nodded. "Crazy thing to miss out on a payday over *that* valuation." I pulled my hair back with a finger, suddenly aware that strands were matting to the back of my neck with sweat.

"I'll say. Anyway, Evanston, he wants to see you. He's in a state, just for your info."

"What about?" I asked. Mural shrugged.

"Crisis aversion? Lamentation? It's not your shit show but he'll put it to you that way for sure."

"Thanks," I said.

"Best of luck, Sue."

"Yeah." Mural waved, his skin turned wan in the office fluorescence, and strode back in the direction of the atrium.

Evanston is a sour lump of carbon on finer days, and so walking then to the reinforced glass door of his office past the duplicated image of his nightmare repeating across every bureau was an exercise in willingness. I rapped on the frosted partition which clicked open for me, revealing Evanston's hulking form hunched over the broad hemisphere of his desk.

"Yeah, Sue, sit," he said, and I moved to an armchair on the opposite wall as the door closed itself behind me. "Well," he said.

"It doesn't make sense."

"It does not, Sue. It does not make sense. I don't need to tell you what we stood to make on this." He rummaged through a drawer looking for something, half-watching a lit panel on the wall adjacent displaying Pollard's address, gave up. "We had federally-granted exclusive licensing on insurance coverage for any potential alien armament of peacekeepers implemented at the state level. That the prime proponent of the bill thinks it's not such a good idea three days before the senate puts it to vote? This fat fuck and his best friend Thee Fat Fuck pull out on the eve of 'Hallelujah'? That is something you can't be taught to predict. That level of bullshit." He leaned back in his chair, staring at me with little eyes beneath heavy folds, through the narrow aperture of his mail-slot spectacles. "I need you to go see him, Sue." I started.

"Pollard?"

"Yeah."

"I do fraud, sir."

"Firstly, I tell you what you do, and also what the fuck is this if not that."

"I mean it's *not* that, it's a disadvantageous turn of events but yeah, okay," I said, "You can define for me my job description. But why would Pollard see me? He doesn't owe us a thing. I'm not some reporter who's gonna spin this for him. What would he say to me?" Evanston clasped his hands across his belly, a portrait of sausage fingers and thinning hair.

"Susan, without elucidating to you unnecessaries, yes he does owe us a thing. And he'll see you."

"Alright," I said, dread inching up my ribs. "So, he'll see me. What do I say?"

"You investigate this like you would a fraud claim," Evanston said. "Put a good face on us. Mine is the last mug he wants to see right now. Come on, Sue. A little charm, a little guile. A little menace. Find out where that fanatical walking slogan of a pundit went so wrong as to run his own fucking bill into the dirt.

"And you can let him know that if we don't get an adequate response, we can make things very difficult for him." He tapped at his desk, flipping off the screen across from him. "You'll take the train up tomorrow morning. We've spoken to his people, they're expecting you."

"Okay."

"That'll be all." I stood. "Oh, and Sue?"

"Yeah?"

"It's a job security thing, you know what I mean?"

Walking outside into evening, beneath the glass mound of the atrium and out through the revolving doors, in the uncomfortable warmth of dusk I encountered sickly Bromund, a Risk Assessment lackey, having a sweaty smoke by himself.

"Hey Sue," he said, as I walked under the floodlights.

"Hey Jon. You got an extra?" He pulled out his pack and shook one out for me.

"How's things?" he asked, lighting my smoke with a cupped hand.

"I dunno. Weird day, for you guys too I'm sure?"

"Yeah, they're breathing on us pretty hard. I guess our projections kinda ate shit on this one." He cleared some phlegm from his throat. "But come on, I can't be the only one in the office that aside from getting needled from above is overwhelmed with joy this thing is maybe not happening anymore." I nodded, blowing smoke above his head into the cone of light. "Like what the cops actually need is a fucking laser rifle to zap some junkie who never finished high school."

"I mean, I don't think it's junkies they're worried about. But no, I'm with you. Fuck in every way the idea of cops with lasers."

Bromund cleared his throat again. "What do you think?" he asked.

"Why Pollard pulled out?"

"Yeah."

"I don't know. Evanston has me on the first train tomorrow to go put it to him."

"No shit?" He ground out his cigarette on the pavement.

"Yeah. And leaves me with some veiled threat as I walk out of his office."

"What a fucking wank. He's just scared, Sue. And talk how he may, he didn't just want this for the contract, he actually wants this."

"Yeah?"

"Yeah. He's not some upwardly mobile benevolent bootstrapper, he's a WASP. He's a fascist not a pragmatist."

"Look at you in a necktie pointing out fascists." Bromund reached reflexively for his throat, let his hand drop back to his side.

"Yeah, well. We can't all be Peacers," he mumbled. I laughed.

"The Peacers would hang you out to dry." He looked down, shame, or some other thing marring his face. "So how come you're working for a fascist, Jon?"

"Show me another kinda boss."

I headed home in an auto-cab under the lights and shadows that follow the evening rush. The windshield displayed Pollard's address, interspersed with footage from the recent violence; some energy discharge rolling through a battalion of riot cops as they fired aimlessly into the night, tumbling together in the tumult, stray ripples of force blowing through the glass barriers of the banking district and sparking fires in their wake. I asked my auto-pilot to turn down the opacity on the news so I could look out at the Potomac rushing by, the neon exuberance of advertisements in the clouds playing off its current. Through the eye of a Prairie Model I could see the moon.

On the train the next morning I settled into my compartment with a PG Tips and a briefcase. I flipped through headlines across the broad window of the vactrain as silver light from the blurred tubing beyond filtered in through images of riots in South Africa; finance details on a studio merger; Pollard and some grumbling senators – Gable, Fredericks and Malone, by the looks of it – as they sat at a press conference a week prior outlining Heaven Forbid to a rowdy knot of press; the President shaking hands with a Tibetan ambassador; a still from video footage of the First Ship plummeting from the sky, hemorrhaging flame and ghostly, part of a series counting down to the 5-year anniversary of Arrival – op eds on our preemptive strike, who they were, why they came, how things could have shaken out differently.

Mural's face popped up over the blasted hull crashing into the Serengeti. "Hey Sue," he smiled weakly. "Glad I caught you. How's things?"

"Fine," I said. "Reading the morning terror."

"Yeah," Mural looked distracted. "Listen, another thing before you get up there."

"I really don't get why I'm being put on this." My tea was getting cold.

"Because we trust you, Sue."

"Bullshit," I laughed. "Evanston's been on my case since Merced fell through, there's no way I'm his first in line to defend against the unthinkable."

39

"Listen to me for a sec, I mean it." Mural hunkered down closer to the camera until I could see the marbling of his eyes and the sharp dip of his cupid's bow, speaking softly and blocking the screen from view of the office. "From me to you, this is... complicated. Evanston's convinced Pollard is in collusion with some outside group. We don't know why... I just, I know you're being sent up there to find answers, and I'm not sure what Evanston is expecting, but Pollard might not be the most receptive right now."

"What does that mean?" I took a sip of tepid tea.

"Just be careful. Get Evanston what he wants and get out of there. Can you link me your location? I know, I feel like I'm overstepping my bounds here, but... just as an insurance policy." I laughed.

"Bad joke."

"Yeah, you keep your head up too, Mural," I lifted the cuff of my jacket to my mouth, miming a wire, "over and out." Mural gave the same weak smile and flipped off the transmission, leaving me to settle back and ponder the molten hunks of jagged debris frozen in the sky above Tanzania as a morning anchor blathered on.

Cracking open the briefcase, I fiddled with the lone tablet inside and flipped my location over to Mural. Letting work keep track of my person was a bit much for me, but they could keep a careful eye on the briefcase, that was just fine. Still trepidatious about meeting the bogeyman of daytime television, I figured maybe there were worse ideas anyway.

The train dragged forward through the tunnel's gleam while anxiety bubbled with cold tea down low in my abdomen.

As we whined into Grand Central I was swept up in the vactrain's evacuation, pulled out the shuddering exit into that wide hall and the patchwork dapple of milky sun through stained glass. Making my way through lurching lines I finally found myself expelled through the double doors out into the

customary midtown bustle, surrounded by haze and lemon light.

Shoving a couple of disgruntled men aside I managed to hail a cab and ducked inside, breathless, shouting "Hackney Building," to the auto-pilot as we whisked away.

Pollard's receptionist was a doleful little woman, an anachronism, a sour troll of rare breed. She sat in a cardigan of grotesque, vivid green behind a desk that dwarfed her. When I shuffled in, attempting to batten down my hair, and asked about my appointment, she fidgeted and dug through the drawers of her desk for reasons I couldn't determine before clasping her hands atop the cluttered bureau and narrowing the gobs of fat around her eyes.

"Yes, Mrs...?"

"Eidelberg," I said. "Miss."

"Mr. Pollard has a number of important meetings this morning, Miss Eidelberg, our office is under a great deal of *duress* at the moment, you see; it is unlikely that Mr. Pollard will find the time – "

"I've just ridden the train up from DC this morning, Miss...?"

"Muller," she sniffed. "Mrs."

"I've just ridden the train up from DC this morning, Mrs. Muller, I'm here representing the Right River Insurance Group and am under direction to speak with Mr. Pollard, who I was told would see me. Our office is also under a great deal of *duress* at the moment, you see. I believe if you check with him you'll find him amenable to my visit. Barring that, grudgingly willing will do." With a withering grimace, she clicked the receiver in front of her.

"Mr. Pollard..."

"Yes, Wendy?" the speaker crackled.

"Someone from Right River here to see you."

•

In the marble breadth of his office, Pollard seemed somehow small behind his desk. His doughy face pocked through with gaping pores, stubby hands folded before him, he lifted one to gesture me in.

"Susan!" he drawled. "Bobby told me you'd be coming. My apologies if Wendy gave you a time, she's been rather dispirited these days." Moving forward, in the time it took me to open a voice memo on my watch, I registered that the alien diminutive "Bobby" must indeed refer to one Robert Evanston, that man in the glass tower above me. As I sat before him, Pollard sighed.

"What can I do for you Susan? I imagine Bobby's not so pleased with me right now."

"Well, no," I said. "Not explicitly." I opened my briefcase in my lap, propping up the tablet and opening a window to take some notes, as I would in a fraud case. "I'm not exactly clear on the nature of your relationship with my employer, Mr. Pollard, but I've been flung up here with no prep to ask you what happened." I smiled.

"What happened?" Pollard repeated, staring at me. "I made an educated, calculated decision Susan, that's what happened. And members of my party agree – "

"Listen, Roman," (I figured as long as we're going by firsts...) "I'm going to level with you, seeing as I've been put in an awkward position here. I was sent up here with very little information, but given the impression that Evanston feels that either you owe him something, or you're reneging on some kind of agreement the two of you have. I've been given the distinct liberty to level veiled threats at you, and tell you that I can make things very difficult for you. I'm not here to get some party line out of you, and I don't think Evanston would be thrilled with that result either. I just need the hard 'why' on your 180 yesterday, and I can't really sit here while

43

you rehash your address on taxation, because despite what you say on the teevee anyone with a modicum of smarts knows you don't give a shit about that." Pollard smirked.

"You'll make things difficult, Susan?" He leaned back in his seat. "Do please tell me how I'm to interpret that."

"You're not a senator anymore, Roman, you're a media man. As I've said, I was sent up here blind and still couldn't tell you why, but as I'm here to bark at you, I'll say Robert Evanston usually does his homework."

"Vultures on all sides," Pollard cooed.

"Point me in the direction of the others and I'll be on my way." Pollard hunkered down on his desk and leaned into me.

"I've only ever had one agenda, Susan. And that is to rid this nation of *filth*." Spittle flecked his lips. "Yes, I smile for the cameras, but not for the likes of you. The wave is coming, Eidelberg." He enunciated my name with a venom. "You'll be swept up. Bobby chooses not to even speak to me direct, he sends some Jew up here to see me? What is this, I ask you? Some facile jest, surely. You tell Bobby I'm stuck. You tell Bobby I know not what to do. Leave my office please."

I dry heaved out on the pavement in the shadow of Hackney's spires. The terse go-getter façade is one I can posture adequately but it ruins my nerves. Sitting inches from that flabby Nazi had me grossly perturbed, and I quivered all over. It is so simple to ignore hatred when you're not near it.

Trembling, I gathered my things and collected myself, turning back into the sun towards the open road where auto-cabs zipped by. I entered one in a heap, requesting Grand Central, and slumped down low in the seat as we buzzed into midtown traffic.

Squishing in some earbuds I pulled up the voice memo on my watch and listened back to our conversation. As the little holo-wheels of tape spun I was thrown by the squeaky sound of my voice, and I sat there dismayed at how little I had actually let Pollard say. The thrust of my anxiety had turned me to a chatterbox, and while I had certainly pushed him around a bit, which was validating, I sat there with the realization that I had left his office with nothing.

I slunk down lower between the imagined mugs of Evanston and Pollard as they mimed gorilla faces above me, rewinding the conversation again and again, my head hanging over my watch. "Vultures on all sides," was what I kept coming back to; he spoke it with a lilt across the narrowband playback. I had quipped back without thinking, but in retrospect my answer had been the correct one. I vaguely threaten blackmail, and he responds with what sounds like a complaint that everyone keeps blackmailing him? Who else then? The Peacers? What lefties scrounged up the scuttlebutt on Pollard?

I needed to return to the Hackney building and put the screws to him, maybe I could extend some false offer of aid. All Evanston wanted from me was an answer, and I was running back with nothing. I pulled myself up to ask for a quick round trip when I realized we weren't in midtown anymore.

"Pilot?" I asked. "Where are you taking me? I need to return to the Hackney building, please." The cab crept into an alley beneath the rearing shade of two buildings. My heartbeat quickened. "Pilot?"

My passenger door wrenched open and black-clad hands bore down on me; I skittered back across the seat to the door opposite, scrabbling at the handle. The figure beat a fist down trying to subdue me, pulling at my legs to wrest me from the cab, and I swung my briefcase into its head. A man's bellow of frustration echoed out into the aluminum ceiling, and I found that the door wouldn't open. A face closed in, he wasn't even masked, white teeth and a five-o-clock shadow. He battered me and I scrunched up back against the door and kicked, closing my eyes as he withdrew a pistol; I kicked again and again filled with the terror of abrupt violence, and futility, awaiting the sound of the gun, when I felt my shoe push into something and stick.

I looked up to see the heel of my pumps extruding from his eye socket, his head hanging limply from my foot. His mouth sagged open; he twitched. I jerked my leg trying to dislodge myself only to push further into his head. Shaking, I screamed.

I let my foot fall and sat there panting, his head nuzzling into my thigh.

"Pilot!" I screamed. There was no answer. Slowly the cab began inching forward, the man's feet scraping along the ground. Panicking, I wriggled, slipped my foot from the shoe, and tumbled over the corpse to spill out into the alleyway, leaving my briefcase and other shoe behind; traipsing barefoot I ran back to the road shouting for help, collapsing in the dripping sun.

From the tumult of it all I hadn't even felt the blows to my head. I lay in the hospital bandaged and bruised, numb to the cursory police questioning. They were brusque, apathetic. The cab with the body had disappeared, and the only signs of struggle were left across my face. I opened up when Ivan called.

"*Mural*," I sighed, his furrowed face staring up from my watch.

"Jesus, Sue, are you okay? What the fuck happened?"

"I don't know. I was attacked. Someone attacked me."

"Shit, what, were you mugged?" I could see the bustle of the office behind him.

"I killed him, Ivan." He sat there silent for a minute. "I wasn't mugged, I was attacked. I killed him."

"Fucking hell. You need to come home, Sue. When can you leave?"

"I'm in fucking insurance, Ivan. I have no stake in this.

What the fuck insurance stiff gets a hit called on them?" Ivan was shaking his head in disbelief.

"Who did this? Any idea?"

"I don't know. The other vultures."

"What?"

"I think Pollard is being blackmailed, that's why he pulled out. Maybe they put out a hit on me, they think I know something? I have no fucking idea. They had control of the cab, it wasn't amateurs. My head *hurts*, Ivan. Fuck." I sank back into the bed. "I just can't see the Peacers or whoever putting out a hit on a civilian." Ivan sat there nodding.

"Just get yourself home, Sue. Get out of the city. Whenever they release you, just come straight home."

In the morning I was let go. They put me in the back of a squad car and drove me to Grand Central, the gummy sun seeping over the pavement. I slept.

"Ma'am?" One of the cops was knocking lightly on the grate between us. "Ma'am, we've arrived. Would you like us to show you to the train?"

"I'll manage," I muttered glumly, my head throbbing. As they drove off I tried to picture their car outfitted in the glowing regalia of alien arms; the dull idiot conferring "ma'am" upon me lugging around a laser rifle.

I called Myra from the train.

"Sweetie!" she exclaimed as her face shimmered into view over the ad-strips. "What in hell, are you alright?" Tears welled up at the corners of my eyes, and though I had meant to nod, I shook my head and scrunched down in my seat, my face wet. "Sue! Where are you, what in the world's going on?" I cleared the tears away, hiccoughed, and sat forward.

"On my way back to DC now. I was fucking *attacked*, My. Some psycho."

"Back to DC from where, what happened? You're okay,

you can get around on your own? Baby! Jesus Christ!"

"From New York, it's a whole fucking story, I'm okay, I can get around, I just, can I come by yours when I get into town? I don't want to go to the apartment and sit there, if I have to watch any more news I'm gonna scream."

"Of course, head straight over! I'll be here waiting."

Myra answered the door in swim trunks and a cardigan, sipping coffee and juggling eyglasses and a tablet, her hair pulled up high. She tried to throw it all down, second guessed, pecked me on the lips and gave me a long hug in the doorframe, the rim of her glasses digging into the back of my neck.

"What the hell, Sue," she breathed. "Come in, come in," she took us into the sitting room and pulled up the blinds as a couple of gleaming drones blurred by; I collapsed into an armchair. "You want coffee?" I nodded. She brought over a cup. "Okay, okay. Tell me what happened."

I got a call from Ivan late in the afternoon while My and I sat smoking, watching a Korean game show in her living room. The volume was low and My was spinning some records off her watch.

"Hey Mural," I answered, his holo face bleeping up above my wrist.

"Sue! Where the hell are you? We've been worried."

"Back in DC," I said. "Convalescing?"

"Are you not coming in? You need to brief us." He raised his eyebrows.

"The hell?" I pointed at my face. "I think I get a sick day."

"Of course you do," he said, nodding. "Of course you do, Sue, I'm sorry. Well, when can we expect you?"

"Mural, there's not much to say. I tried to bully him, it didn't work and that was the end of it. And I'm putting my money on blackmail. I'll be in before the end of the week."

"Alright, well, Evanston's on a tear and wants to speak with you. Sooner the better. Sorry to keep throwing you to him like this, but don't shoot the messenger."

"He's a big boy, Ivan, tell him to call me."

"We'll see you when you're feeling up to it, Sue. In the meantime stay home and rest up." Ivan tried to smile.

"Yeah, you too. Work-related injuries shouldn't include ulcers."

"Very funny."

"Over and out."

That night Myra ordered Thai and we ate on the couch and I could barely keep my eyes open.

"Dunno what to do," I lamented, slopping down flat noodles.

"Work wants you back in," said My, reclining. I nodded. "What do you want?"

"I dunno," I said. "Uncharacteristic." I scrunched my aching face. "Part of me just wants to know who that fucking ape was." She looked up at me. "I could smell his cologne, My. Is it too weird that I just want to know who bothers to get dignified before they go woman-killing?" Myra looked at me, noncommittal. "I've got his brains on my pumps. Is it unreasonable that I want to know his name?"

"What did he look like? Did you get a good look?"

"He looked like a white guy. He looked like any guy you'd see walking down the street making 80k at an investment firm, slurping a coffee and patting a messenger bag. Had like a manicured 5 o'clock shadow. German or Irish or something. The guy your mom wants you to date before you come out of the closet." Myra sat up, nodding.

"Gimme your real best guess. Who do you think did it?" I shook my head.

"I really don't know. I don't know who. But someone's blackmailing Pollard, that's the only explanation for him backing off Heaven Forbid, and I think whoever's blackmailing *him* thinks that *I* know, and wants me gone."

"You think Pollard knows who?"

"He's got to," I sighed.

"It's like high school, but your face is all fucked up."

"No, you're right, it's exactly like high school." Myra lit a smoke and sat by the window, every now and then a drone banking by in the moonlight.

"So let me just follow the line of this," she said, ashing into the night. "Pollard." I nodded. "One-time Republican Majority Leader, senator from Oklahoma." I kept nodding. "The aliens come." She gestured about her head. "They put themselves over Tanzania, Papua New Guinea, Nepal, Honduras, Bolivia, we still don't know why these of all places."

"Yeah."

"Pollard uses his pull, gets together with Pres. and the Pentagon, creates a military coalition with Russia, China, everybody we say we hate."

"Yeah."

"We still haven't heard a peep from the aliens, military moves in on the Tanzanian ship which is over the least populated area, and they blow it out of the sky in a show of strength. There is no fight. They just shoot a bunch of bullshit at it and blow it up. The other ships leave."

"Yeah."

"Everybody fights to pick through the rubble. Pollard resigns in a shitstorm of controversy from humanitarian and environmentalist groups, rides his notoriety into celebrity. Within a year alien tech has leaked to the streets, bolsters the largest group of domestic terrorists we've ever seen, and Pollard speaks up to right the wrongs of the preemptive strike, though not exactly posited like that. Throws all his weight behind some trendy legislation. Somebody blackmails him. He backs off it. A white guy wearing bad cologne tries to kill my best friend in a cab."

"*Yeah.*"

Myra hiked her knee up and looked out at the city, shaking her head.

"What are you gonna do, Sue?"

"Pollard knows who did this. I gotta go back. Right? Go arm wrestle with that fucking secretary again and get another meeting with him."

"You gonna tell Right River?"

"Nah. Either they'll never know, or I find what I need and they'll be elated."

"Stay here tonight?"

"Yeah. Thanks."

"And do me a favor?"

"Anything." Myra stubbed out her smoke on the window sill and moved across the house, disappearing into her bedroom. Her voice muffled:

"Take this with you?" She reemerged carrying a pistol, an old snub-nose like from the movies. She held it in her palm, cocky.

"Are you fucking kidding me," I laughed, almost slipping from the couch. "Myra Watts. Owns a *handgun*. I never knew you."

"Oh shut up. It's a fucking antique. But it works. And the next time Eau Sauvage comes knocking you won't have to put your shoe through his head."

"You are too much." My words caught in my throat.

"Take it?" She moved over to me, welling up.

"Thank you, My." She put her arms around me.

"I swear to God if some Giorgio Armani motherfucker..." I laughed into her chest, my throat straining.

"I love you, My."

"I love you, Sue."

I went to bed on the couch.

•

In a dream there were foil palm trees. Fronds gleamed shrilly in the sun, as jeweled baubles on a trade wind, white with heat. In the sky was a pattern of blue flesh, rippling as if newly smattered by rain, and in the eddies of sapphire gooseflesh I saw the most vivid depiction, marches of madness circumscribed by starlight. Then a hit, as if from a piano key, and a tremor thundered across the ocean of skin.

Myra shook me awake as the sun was crawling over the skyline and pointed to the TV. News alerts were bleeping on my watch and I could see the same headlines flitting over Myra's tablets and across the heavy clouds outside:

"Roman Pollard Dead, Suspected Murder"
"Roman Pollard Found Dead at Hackney Building"
"Media Mogul Pollard Killed at 62"
"Police Investigate Death of Ex-Senator Roman Pollard"

I sat up groggy, winced at a twinge in my ribs, and glared blearily at the screen, my head throbbing.

"The fuck," was all I managed.

"I know," said My, banging a coffee down in front of me. "The fuck for real."

She stopped me in her doorway.

"You're not still going?"

"I'm still going."

"Sue, he's dead! He can't tell you anything."

"Then I'll see what I can find on my own. Fuckers almost got me, My, and then they got him...! I don't want to stay here, get you wrapped up in this. And anyway you gotta admit, the last place I'll be in danger is the damn crime scene!"

"You're delirious."

"I am wide awake!"

·

After taking leave of Myra I decided to head back to my apartment to wash up and change before catching an early train back to the city. I moved to hail a cab, thought better of it, and hopped on a bus. On the way back to my building I flipped around on my watch and did some research to find that, as I suspected, Right River handled a life insurance policy for Pollard. Hoping that they hadn't already sent someone in an official capacity this early in the game, that would be my in. If I wasn't the first to arrive I could always feign confusion, a posture I can generally execute more deftly than that of the bad cop anyhow.

Walking the last couple blocks to my building I slumped into the elevator and whirred up to my floor, waltzing down the hall to my unit. I walked inside and shut the door behind me before I realized something was off. The deadbolt hadn't been locked. I always lock the deadbolt.

I reached deep in my jacket pocket to squeeze the grip of the snub-nose nestled in the crevice of fabric, my palms sweating. A ripple of blue flesh passed across my periphery, a migrainous starburst, and for reasons I could not at the time comprehend, I dropped to one knee as I turned to face my apartment. A sizzle passed above my head, scorching the air above me and I was suddenly awash in the stench of burnt hair as I found myself gaping at another average white man, this one clad in a backpack and athletic wear, holding in his outstretched hand the distinct agglomeration of lumpy alloy indicative of alien tech, the edge of its nozzle shimmering with the heat of discharge. Before I could think, I shot him in the chest.

The kick of the muzzle sent me back into the door, the shot deafening in my small apartment. The man scrambled back, clutching at his ribs, between his fingers a smile of red. I was kaput on the floor trying to blink away the stars, the scent of gunpowder and hair and cyan flesh, a haze of salt and carbon, but looked up to the see the man in a panic, hemorrhaging, and grasping behind his ear. He tugged, frantic, and tugged again, and his body blinked from view. I sat there in a daze, wondering if my brain had lapsed. He was gone, with nothing but a spatter of blood left behind.

I didn't even think, I just climbed back to my feet and ran from the apartment, fled downstairs to the street. A bus was waiting at the stop when I arrived, about to leave, and I scurried to the doors waving my arms like a psychopath and climbed aboard.

Before I knew it I was back on the vactrain to NY, staring at images of Pollard's face scrolling across the viewing panes. In his doughy visage I was shocked by my own reflection, an artist's array of purples and yellows spawning across my face, my right eye puffed to a softball, and now a flat angled swatch of hair atop my head, burnt off as if with a level. I decided to powder my nose at Grand Central.

In the yawning enclosure of that milky hall, I stood in the bustle and tried to catch my breath. Though I looked like a wellness clinic escapee, thankfully this was still New York, and no matter the year or season I forever might as well be wallpaper. I trundled into the washroom and splashed a stinging rinse of water across my face; blew my nose like a foghorn, leaning my head into the marble wall, and cried for just less than an instant.

Straightening my overcoat, I gave myself a sassy look in the mirror. It would take a while to find my way about the city without an auto-cab, and time was of the essence; I needed to go lie to some people, and look at the blasted body of a terrible man.

•

A lurid fleet of police vehicles flanked the cold flagstones of the Hackney building, the buzzing blues and reds painting the morning purple with anxiety. The stone toad of an officer standing before the front doors eyed me with suspicion as he lapped at the soggy rim of a cardboard mug.

"May I help you, Miss?" he asked, straining his voice over the bustle. At curbside a half dozen reporters yammered away into cameras, their voices spread to the air through the vaulted antennae raised from the rooftops of as many hastily parked news vans.

"Susan Eidelberg," I said, waving my ID for him. "Here from Right River, representing the deceased."

"Right River?" he asked, his face sagging.

"Representing the deceased," I repeated. His eyes drifted up to my impromptu haircut.

"I can't say's they'll want you in there," he muttered, "but go on up."

Another man worthy of a laser rifle, I noted to myself as I climbed the stairs.

Pollard's reception was abuzz with investigators, chattering and chuckling and waving their pens about in distress. Wendy Muller stood in a corner, her face white with shock, chalky above her vomitous emerald sweater. I moved over to her, and watched as her eyes adjusted from behind me to somewhere at my throat.

"Hello, Mrs. Muller." She stared at me blankly. "Susan Eidelberg, from Right River."

"Oh yes," she said. "The Jewish girl from insurance."

"Like some beast of nightmare," I said smiling. "Can you tell me anything about what happened?" She stood there sullenly, and her eyes filled with tears.

"I can't speak of it," was all that came out. "The horror, the horror..." She looked rather small, lost in the fuss of uniforms and blather.

"I'm sorry for your loss," I said. She stared up at me,

envenomed, and I could hear her quiet words through the ruckus:

"In one hundred years you will be buried in an unmarked grave, unremembered; your soul will sit at whatever seat in hell is reserved for the godless." I stared back. "Roman's vision will shine forever. They will build statues of Roman. Our Father will welcome him with arms reserved for the beloved. On the final day of days when you are left in the ground, Roman will be there, and he will welcome me back into the light."

I gulped, my heart hammering. From behind me I heard someone ask, "Who is that?"

"I'll see you there with the aliens," I said to her, my face a mask.

Again from behind, "Excuse me Miss, who are you?"

"I'll be the one eating pussy and saying the Kaddish." A hand fell on my shoulder. "Maybe not at the same time," I smiled, turning around. "Hello! Susan Eidelberg, Right River Insurance, I'm here on behalf of the deceased."

I stood facing a broad, bearded man, small eyes pushed close around a flat nose, their gaze drifting over my arrangement of bruises.

"Ah, I see," he said, taken aback. "Unfortunately, Miss Eidelberg, this is, ah, still a crime scene as you can see, and as you're not directly involved with the investigation I must ask you to leave the premises for the time being."

"I'm sorry, I should have introduced myself before talking to Mrs. Muller here. And you are?"

The man cleared his throat. "Special Investigator Robert Fulton. Shall I escort you downstairs?"

"That won't be necessary, Mr. Fulton," I said cordially. "For security reasons this investigation will soon be under federal purview, I'm sorry you're not fully apprised. Right River is a private organization, but we do report directly to the Bureau with our findings regarding any fatal case involving current or former government employees. This is a bit more high profile than we're accustomed to as you might imagine, I really just need to take some photos and speak to a few of Pollard's personnel so my employers can be made fully aware of the situation before the next team arrives. If you have any questions feel free to reach out to Right River, I'm sure they can answer them for you."

The man clucked and bristled. "This is the first I've heard of any of this. It's highly unorthodox to allow a private agent on the premises of a crime scene."

I took my identification from a breast pocket. "If it makes you more comfortable," I proffered it to him. "You're cooperation will be *greatly* appreciated. I assure you it won't take more than a moment."

"Miss, may I ask if you're feeling alright?" He handed back my ID and made a gesture that seemed to refer to the whole of me.

"Quite fine, thank you. The sooner I get started the sooner I can leave."

Pollard sat in his cushioned leather chair, which had rolled back to touch the far wall. His head was splayed open, the threads of his throat stretching like upended tree roots to meet the black scorch marks rising up along the wall behind him. He looked relaxed, almost. Bits of meat clung to his tie and the room was filled with a sloppy joe stench of cooked flesh.

A forensics team circled the vanitas like dancers, wheeling around with cameras and robin's egg shoe coverings, the muffled scuff of polypropylene and the clack of shutters garbling to a whisper. Several men glanced in my direction but most paid me no mind. I felt as though I too should take photos, though I wasn't sure why. My head began to spin, the microwave stench of Pollard's disassembled face rolled over me and I was overcome with a wave of nausea.

Why was I here? I needed information from a dead man. He was gone, and yet his leaving hadn't altered my course of action; rather I had fled from DC with still greater haste. I stared at Pollard's dribbling carcass. Somehow that emanation of hate I had felt sitting across from him a day before, the hate that had made me wretch in the street, it had not dissipated. A despicable man met a dreamt-of fate, and yet it felt to me there was no less hate in the world. I felt doubly ill.

Several members of the forensics team had begun to stare at me. Feeling the need to perform some professional action I fumbled down for a briefcase that wasn't there.

My briefcase.

It's funny, but in almost losing my life twice in the last 24 hours, I had all but forgotten it.

Awkwardly I turned, and stumbled from the room back into the bustle of the reception area. Fulton was speaking to a colleague and gesturing toward me as I emerged. I put my head down and hurried for the exit, their eyes following me as I left.

Walking quickly down the hall, as I approached the stairs I heard a sob escape through a door cracked ajar. Slowing my gait, I approached, curious.

Through the narrow gap I saw a large man hunched over in his chair, bawling silently into huge soft hands. He was squeezed into an ill-fitting expensive suit, white at the knuckles and red with strain everywhere else. The hands slipped down his wet face with a sucking sound and red eyes stared up to meet mine through the cracked door. I stared at him blankly until it registered; he looked so strange without his makeup.

The Big Fat Idiot looked out into the hall at me, not uninviting; and with legs that felt as though they belonged to another I stepped confidently through the door and shut it behind me.

"Hello," he mustered, staring up at me with some confusion. We were in a small office with a view facing the building adjacent, a reflection of cool concrete light from the windows turned yellow by an odious lamp in the corner. The Big Fat Idiot sat in a chair that seemed positioned for a visitor, quivering.

"Hello," I tried to smile. "My name is Susan, I'm here from the Right River Insurance group, representing Mr. Pollard." I extended my hand.

He wiped some clammy residue off on a pant leg before extending his own. "Rupert Weber," he said. "I work with Roman. Worked," he shuddered, and looked down as though he were about to vomit, kneading his jaw with a flat thumb.

"I believe I've seen you on television," I said, pulling up a chair across from him. He tried to smile as well. "I'm very sorry for your loss."

Rupert nodded. "I just can't believe it. I can't." He steadied a hand on his chest and took a breath before going on. "He was just here. We shared a meal yesterday afternoon." I nodded back.

"Can you tell me anything about what happened?"

"I don't know much," he said, speaking to his shoes. "It must have happened first thing in the morning, or sometime last night if he stayed at the office late. He never ca—" he cut himself off, raising red eyes to me like a child in the wrong. "The last I saw of him was when I left the office yesterday evening."

"I see. Please, go on," I urged him softly, though I believed he had most likely just told me the biggest piece there was to tell.

"When I arrived this morning he was already— he was already—" A gurgle sounded from somewhere in his chest, and the grief he had caged in my presence was swept out in a wave of fluid. I felt bereaved, ashamed, sitting there staring

59

at him. In some misplaced effort of empathy I stood and moved to him, but he held a hand up, mumbling, "Please." I sat back down across from him as he took a handkerchief from his breast pocket and spread the square across his face. A painting of orifices soaked through the linen. When he had recomposed himself, he continued. "Wendy found him when she came in this morning. Found him like that. *Who*, in God's name..." he gripped the leather beneath him.

"That's what I'm trying to discover, Rupert." I leaned back, exhausted, closing my bruised eyelids.

"We all know who," he muttered. I looked up at him, and he at me, eyes rimmed red with fire. "Those punks. Fucking commie street garbage with lasers."

"But he just backed off the legislation, Rupert, why would they kill him now?" He held up his hands exasperated.

"A mystery. They have no principles, maybe that's the long and short of it. Motherless scum." His hands fell to his sides, and he sagged. I stood, moving to the door, and again, in a spasm, saw blue.

"Thank you for your time, Rupert. You're a wonderful entertainer. May you yet find further joy in your work."

Out on the street I moved away from the Hackney building and sank down onto the curb in the sun. So Pollard was fucking the Idiot. I had a miserable headache.

I was no closer to knowing who had blackmailed Pollard, who had killed him, who was trying to kill me, or for that matter whether any of those were in fact the same party. I did, however, know the tea, for whatever that was worth.

And now the forgotten briefcase was my only lead. I flipped around listlessly on my watch – more headlines about Pollard bleeping from every holo-corner of innerspace – before coming to the little radar app that let me track devices with an open location. Finding the tablet registered to me, I pulled up the geo-sig to find it was still in the city. Just across town. Again eyeing the auto-cabs warily, I decided to walk.

It was a hot day, as all the days had been; and though my face stung unpleasantly, the city sun brought some feeling back into the rest of me. My overcoat hung low on me, unnecessary, but I kept it on with a hand on the snub-nose in the pocket. Occasionally my watch would bleep some nonsense at me, but I paid no mind; drifting along the stinking pavement I sank into an ill-conceived feeling of peace, a trance of exhaustion that left behind ideas of where I was headed or why I headed there. For some three quarters of an hour I managed to take a nice walk in New York.

Eventually I turned into a grayer neighborhood. Pedestrians dissipated and I found myself walking past the chain-link fences of bus depots, tattered razor wire drooping like vines. Semis were lined up beneath the shade of a yawning overpass, and a couple men stood smoking in the street. I checked my watch to find I was almost on top of the signal. My heart fluttered.

Around the bend I went to find two large doors of corrugated iron, shut and padlocked. I stood outside an unremarkable building, an industrial warehouse the color of pavement. I pushed my hands up against the doors expecting something, a feeling, I wasn't sure what. I felt nothing. Stepping back into the street I looked up, as if I could find the answer by taking measure of the place.

The building took up most of a city block, and faint overlapping outlines of grime mapped out the shape of old insignias, a P, an S, vaguer shapes scrawled out in the mottled dust. A drone banked by overhead as I made my way down a long block of abandoned cars, their distended tires flopping out over the pavement, dashboards covered in trash.

Coming to the southern side of the building I found a rickety fire escape patinated like blue coral, ramping along a

61

set of windows opaque with dust. I turned in a slow circle. There was no one around. Faintly I could hear the hum of something mechanized from an adjacent factory. I hauled over a nearby dumpster, hoping the clangor was nothing unprecedented around here, and climbed atop to find that with a leap I could just reach the lowest rung of the ladder. I scrambled up with a gasp and heaved myself onto the first landing.

Quietly I crept up level by level. Dirt was caked across the windows obscuring any view of the interior, but a harsh glare caught my eye and I saw near the top a single pane wedged open, angled into the sun. Up and up I went, sweating through my overcoat, until finally I scrabbled onto the top landing and hunched down near the open pane, breathless. Peering through, it looked as though it opened onto some kind of catwalk among the rafters. I pulled at the pane, and it swung out with a juddering. Taking a deep breath, I poked my head through.

First everything was dark. Then dimly in the murk I could make out a vast open space, a decommissioned hangar of some kind. Balconies ran along the walls at different levels, with catwalks running out from them to a central terminus of scaffolding. Withdrawing my head, I slid the window open another foot until I thought I might fit, and before I could think better of it, climbed through.

Blind and grasping, I had to blink away the sun from outside again until my eyes adjusted. I could barely breathe through the dust in the air. Crouching down, I began inching forward as quietly as I could; slow and low I crept along the catwalk, throwing up veils of dust with each movement, every shift of my weight a disruption to an ancient film of ashen skin and a million dead spiders. I covered my mouth with a jacket sleeve and stayed the course, until after an indeterminate period of time I heard a muffled voice, and noticed movement below. Someone was pacing at ground level, just around the wall of scaffolding. My heart in my throat, I crept forward until the figure came into view.

Another unremarkable white guy paced around a yellow auto-cab, talking down into his watch. That was my cab, I was sure of it. Barely breathing, choked with dust, I strained my ears to hear:

"... yes, we can have the cab back out on the street by end of day. I took care of the mess. Would you like me to send the remains to the family or should I dispose of them?"

"We'll have to dispose of them," a tinny voice rang out from the man's watch. A shard of ice slipped into my brain; the voice was achingly familiar, but I couldn't place it. "We'll need to deny any knowledge of death."

"The girl left some belongings in the cab."

"Yeah, her location is still reading over there. Throw them in with the body. We need everything demolecc'ed. In fact, zap it all now to be safe, we don't want anyone looking for the tablet." The man nodded, and leaned back against the scaffolding, throwing his watch call up on the cab window with a swipe. "Thanks for running over there on short notice," said Ivan Mural from the window.

My world went sideways. For a moment, all I could do was panic. I lay there gulping down mouthfuls of dust. A gap opened between myself and my understanding of things, how everything fit, and I froze, staring across the gulf. Finally, on the verge of arrest, I sneezed.

The man tensed and looked up to the distant rafters, his brow furrowed.

"Something wrong?" asked Mural from the window.

"Not sure," he answered, his gaze steady on my position. "Thought I heard something."

"Well, go check it out for peace of mind," Mural said, distracted by something behind him. "But 'til recently no one'd gone in that place in a decade, we just own the building. I'm sure it's overrun with vermin."

"Yeah," said the man, turning back to Ivan. I started making back for the windows, crawling on my belly so as to be invisible from the lower vantage. "What's next, when I'm finished here?"

"We have to find Eidelberg," I heard Mural say; I stopped in my tracks. "She's armed. Andrews tried to hit her at her apartment and she shot him. We've got him in ICU now, he almost didn't make it."

"*Two* down," the man replied. "Not such an incapable stiff, then. Do we think she's the Peacer mole?"

"We still don't know," Ivan sighed. I started moving again, cautiously, the voices receding as they disappeared beyond the far wall of scaffolding. "Probably. The fact is, it doesn't make a difference, we just need Capitol Hill to think Pollard was in bed with them and that's why he pulled out. As long as they buy that, they'll tack on our exclusivity to whatever the new bill is. If she is the mole, then we got her, if she's not then we have a body, and with her record it'll be easy for them to connect whatever dots we give them. Believe it or not they still don't like Jews on the Hill." In my terror, I almost laughed. There was a longer pause, and for a minute neither man spoke. "We've just had a call from someone on the Pollard case." Mural sounded tense. "They'd like to know if a Susan Eidelberg was sent up there to represent us this morning. I need you to run over to the Hackney building, talk to anyone there, see if you can retrace her steps. We really can't afford to have her running around."

"Alright. I'll head over there now and see what I can do, but talk to someone at TelSoft, see if you can get a read on her watch. Just say it's national security."

"They'll never listen to me."

"Then have the cops do it, tell them they just let a suspect into their crime scene..."

By now I was almost at the windows and firmly out of the man's sight. As quietly as I could I hauled myself clumsily

back over the precipice, my foot stuck for a moment on the lip of the sill, and then I was free, back in sunlight.

I hurried down the fire escape, dropped down onto the black plastic dumpster lid, pliant in the heat, and tumbled to the pavement. Without a coherent thought in my head, I booked it down the street.

When I thought my lungs would burst, I stopped, doubling over. It was early evening now, and I flopped down in an alley and dropped my throbbing head into my hands, watching the brilliant sun roll down the walls. The pain in my chest was so great I couldn't even get the air down, and before I knew it I was crying and I couldn't stop. It came up in great gasping sobs, and I drooled all over myself like a child. I had never felt so singularly poised over the great black pit; a yawning hate-hole above which I hovered.

When the wracking sobs abated I slipped my watch off my wrist and smashed it into the concrete over and over until it was barely an object. Then I pulled my heels up to my butt, pushed my eyes to my knees, pulled my overcoat over my head, and huddled there, rocking, straining to feel the warmth of the setting sun. I lost track of time.

In some stretch of my fever pit I heard the clack of footsteps as someone passed by the alley, then stopped in front of me. Raising my head, I looked up to the alley entrance, shielding my eyes from the orange sun. A man stood there, backlit, and I couldn't make out a face.

"Sue," he said. It wasn't a question. I scrabbled back and jumped to my feet, as he moved forward into the alley. I geared up to run, and as he stepped into shadow my eyes adjusted to his face.

"Bromund?" He smiled at me. "Don't fucking come any closer." I pulled out the snub-nose and clocked it at his face, brushing tears from my eyes with a sleeve.

"Hey Sue," he held up his hands, palms out. "I'm not

here to hurt you. For real." I didn't lower the gun.

"Fucking right," I said. "Everyone has my best interests at heart." He looked mildly pathetic, sweating through his crumpled office attire. Slowly he reached toward a pant pocket. "Don't fucking do it, Bromund, I am so sick to death of killing office boys. Just leave me the fuck alone, I will leave and I will never come back, whatever you want I swear to god."

"Sue..."

"Look, I wanted to know who was after me – now I know! I am just a girl with a shitty job out of college that I never left, I so have no stake in this, please just leave me the fuck alone!" I screamed, and it echoed past him out into the street.

"You want a smoke?" He pulled a pack from his pocket. My arm wavered. "I am really not here to hurt you, Sue. I know that seems unlikely given the things you've just heard, but I am really not here to hurt you. I am not with Right River. Have a smoke."

"What do you mean you're not with Right River?" I kept the gun trained on his nose.

"I am not with Right River." A drone circled past, overhead, and he pointed up to it. "We've been monitoring their properties. I know this is all a misunderstanding, I know you're not the Peacer mole."

"How do you know that?"

"Because I am." Sickly Bromund. He put a cigarette between his lips and lit up, then raised his hands again. Haltingly, I lowered the gun. "Sue, please, have a smoke." He blew a cone out over my head. "Let's not talk in the street."

It was the best cigarette I'd ever had. A real humdinger of a cigarette. We sat in a slick black Acura as it slid down side streets. It was a self-driver, but I asked him to keep his hands on the wheel for my peace of mind.

"Where are we going?" I asked.

"Doesn't matter. This is your life and you're the boss. I can make suggestions."

"Can you just tell me what the hell is going on?"

"We don't really know. Some big moves are happening, it's unclear who's behind them."

"That is the least helpful sentence in the world, Bromund."

"My name is Matthew," he said sticking out his hand. "Matthew Howard." I shook it.

"Great to finally meet you." I felt ill. "Bromund is a fucking Peacer mole," I said to myself. "Why is there a fucking Peacer mole at Right River?"

"Howard."

"Okay Howard. Pull over, I'm gonna be sick."

We pulled into an alley behind a line of shuttered vendors and I dry heaved out the door for a minute. I slouched back into the car feeling woozy and the terrorist spy from Risk Assessment offered me a water from the backseat. I took a long glug.

"Can you just start from the beginning?" I asked, wiping my mouth.

"What's the beginning?" I sat back, thinking.

"Arrival."

"Well," he laughed. "We don't know too much more than anyone else. Five ships showed up, we shot down the cell over Tanzania, and the rest fled. The official line is still that no bodies were recovered from the wreckage, only tech. We know nothing about them. Whoever arrived. But eventually that tech made its way to the black market, and that made it possible for our ramshackle operation to get off the ground."

"Did the Peacers predate arrival?"

"Well, no. But the sentiment did. I mean, you know." He lit another smoke, sweating. "Things have been bad for a very long time. There's a lot of hate in the world." I took a long look at Matthew Howard. "We just use their shit. We don't know anything about them." He sat back, his shirt matting to the seat, then shook his head. "Actually, no, that's not true. One thing most people probably don't know is that the tech we all use wasn't derived from artillery. At least that's what I've been told by people who've been involved since the get-go. It's transport technology we've jerry-rigged." I laughed. "So do with that what you will. But one could extrapolate that they didn't come here to eat us, if nothing else." I slouched forward, and supported my head on an open palm.

"So you're really the bogeyman," I said, staring at him. "What the hell do you people want?"

"We're pretty public about our desires," he said, tilting his head. "We want a redistribution of resources. There is enough wealth concentrated among literal individuals in this country to feed, clothe and house the world. We want an end to the police state. An end to drone strikes, the war economy. First World profiteering over the destabilization of smaller nations. Ethnic cleansing funded by the West. Wall Street."

"And you think killing cops is the way to do that?"

"Fuck cops," he said flatly.

"Fair enough."

"I'm not here to convert you," he said, flipping his cigarette out the window. "I'm just here to get you off the street."

"Did you guys blackmail Pollard?"

"No."

"Did you guys kill Pollard?"

"No."

"Then what the fuck *is* all this?" I slapped a hand at the glove box, exasperated.

"That is all I have spent the last two days trying to figure out. And to answer your earlier question, I was placed at Right River two years ago to monitor the situation. It's no secret you guys have ties to the Hill. But I am right there with you Sue, and honestly I was hoping you might be able to help me out. Someone is fucking with us, all of us. This all lines up way too perfectly to look like a Peacer job. Right River *wants* it to be, for Christ's sake. But they still would have obviously preferred that the bill just pass, so there's no way they did it. I just don't know." He laid his palms on the steering wheel, thrumming his fingers on the rim.

"Well I don't know a fucking thing, Bromund," I laughed.

"Howard."

"Howard. I don't know anything, Howard."

"What about the guys who tried to off you?"

"Actually, yeah," I said, nodding. "The first guy was just a gorilla, but the second guy shot at me with some kind of laser. And he fucking teleported."

"He what?"

"He yanked on his ear and he teleported. Hand to god." Howard stared down, thinking. "So I guess that is some kind of remarkable."

"So Right River has tech," he said, looking up at me.

"I mean it's just on the black market, no? I think Right River just has money."

"It's not just readily available, Sue. Not like they've tried to make it seem."

"Well where did you guys get it?"

"I can't tell you that," he laughed. I stared at him. "I don't know," he said, raising his eyebrows. "To be totally frank." I sighed.

"Well," I grabbed his cigarettes off the seat and lit another. "Where do we go from here, Matthew Howard?"

"If you're open to suggestions, I would advocate we get out of the city. We can find a motel for the night, and figure out a better game plan for you in the morning."

"A motel? You guys don't have like a stronghold or something?" He side-eyed me. I shrugged.

"I really think leaving the city right now is best. Have you ever had any invasive surgeries, any implants?" I shook my head. "And you ditched your watch?"

"Yeah."

"Alright, buckle up. I hear it's beautiful in Putnam this time of year."

Matthew was a quiet roommate. When we got to the motel he washed up, checked the mattresses for bugs, and undressed in a corner.

"Would you like to watch TV?" he asked.

"More than anything I would like to sleep."

In the trickling quiet of that small musty room, I weighted myself beneath a horizon of polyester sheets and fell to the murk as though dead.

A sky smattered with stars rose high above the jagged shore, briny hands of gauze lapping in a taught breeze. A pigeon the color of night leapt from a broken tree to hurl itself at the dark. My footprints, trailing back, were the shape of starfish, and in each comb of surface were shimmering sheaves, accretions of silver.

In the gloaming, a moaning of light crested the stretched sea, and as the sky bleached with warmth the great belly of blue gooseflesh made itself a spectacle, yawning above like a wavering tide. Gleaming baubles mounted the wind and rode up to meet it, vaulting from each twig and small purchase, a heraldry of silver in the air.

Quivering, I stood, a lone specimen on the beach. The sky-skin was at once mother, and lover.

On some arc of dream my hands, my feet, yes, they were starfish, starfish!

When I woke in the morning I told Matthew I knew what we had to do.

71

"We can't go back," he said, stirring instant coffee into a plastic mug. "Or we very much shouldn't. I haven't shown at work, most likely my cover's blown. They'll think we were working together the whole time."

"We're not going back to Right River, Matthew, we're going back to the Hackney." He laughed.

"I'm in hiding now too, Sue, which means my communication is limited; so the resources at my disposal are as well. We need to go *away* from New York. There are places, obviously, that we have. Where we can be more than safe."

"I don't care about being safe, Matthew." I sat back on the bed.

"Says the 'I just got this job out of college please leave me alone' girl."

"I saw it in a dream." All the air went out of him.

"Oh for fucking Christ's sake not you too." He plopped down on the bed adjacent, his head in his hands.

"I know it sounds like trash," I said smiling. I could smell the blue skin, I felt it beneath my nails. "But it's wonderful." Howard sat there shaking his head, and he started to laugh. "Wait, what do you mean not me too?"

"You've really never been in contact with another Peacer?"

"I've really never. Not to my knowledge."

"This is a real whacko turn here," he said. He pulled out a smoke, moved to a window and cracked it. He stared into the warm sun that peered in, puffing. "We've been having issues. For a while." I sat there staring at him. "No one's gone rogue exactly, or anything like that. They're just... interpreting orders differently."

"They're dreaming?" He nodded. I curled up and was subsumed for a moment in the brightest glee. "Matthew," I said, breathless. "I want to follow it."

"Yeah, you all want to follow it."

"What do you think it is?"

"Russia for all I fucking know. What do *you* think it is?"

"I think it's one of them," I said. He looked at me. "I think one of them stayed behind."

It was a long drive back to New York, and Matthew was unhappy. He threw his watch into the woods along the roadside just to be safe, and pretended he didn't care. As it turns out, communists can have affinity for their possessions too.

As we drove I tried to explain the language of the dream, and found that I couldn't. He asked me several times what we would be looking for, and at first I was unsure how to answer. And yet with each refrain of the question I was pulled back to the dream, and in those gasping moments where my stomach would fall away, I found that there were kernels of information.

By the time we reached the Harlem River, I had something I could verbalize.

"There's a camera."

"A camera?"

"In his office."

"Sue, I hope you have something better than that." We crawled to a halt at a traffic light. Matthew hadn't stopped smoking for an hour. "Because if it's a camera in his office, then the cops have already found it. There's just no way."

"They haven't found it."

Matthew had a small store of cash, and we ate lunch at a bodega and decided to kill time until it got dark. We sat in his car and I asked him questions and we smoked lots of cigarettes. I got us coffee twice, and my nerves were a tattered jest by the time the sun went down.

We parked several blocks from the Hackney building out of some ambient paranoia. It wasn't like we had a getaway driver anyhow. Before heading over, Matthew circled around to the Acura's trunk and popped it open. Inside were a series of straps and divots cradling an array of ridged and nozzled equipment, straddled like iron children. I looked over to him with a brow crease.

"How were you planning on getting inside?" he asked. He hefted up a wide-barreled mechanism cased in fissured copper with a grip wrapped in rubber. It smelled of sulfur and battery acid.

"I guess I hadn't thought," I said, staring at the contraption. "What is that thing?"

"A quantum tunneler," he said, running a scrap of cloth from the trunk along the apertures down the barrel. "It'll scramble somebody's insides. And lower molecular density."

"So we're gonna...?"

"Walk through the wall." He grabbed another smaller hand-device and tucked it in his belt. I looked at him again. "Stunner."

He threw on an overcoat and tucked the tunneler inside, under his arm. We walked around the block and ducked into an alley adjacent the Hackney. Matthew turned to me.

"Okay," he said, reaching into his jacket. "When we're doing shit for real everyone gets their own EM widget. But this wasn't supposed to be that, and I don't have any." He handed me a ski mask. I took it into my hands and stared at it, gripping the knit. He shrugged at me and pulled one over his own head. I followed suit.

We jogged through the alley around to the backside of the Hackney. The surrounding offices were all long-closed, and the street was empty. Except for a few twinkling windows in firms high above us and the occasional whir of a passing auto-cab there was no sign of anyone around.

We approached the rear entrance. We could see through the glass double doors that the security desk around this side was empty. Matthew hurried up to the wall adjacent, withdrew the tunneler and pressed the nozzle up to the marble. He depressed the trigger and caught the recoil in his shoulder as a muffled 'UMP' sounded against the stone. Without a backward glance he pushed his way in, as though fighting some kind of resistance.

"Hurry after," was all he muttered before disappearing into the rock.

I took a deep breath, held my hands up in front of my face, took a couple steps back to try to get some momentum, and pushed forward. I hit the flat plane like a bellyflop. It was like swimming through gelatin; the cold surface cut its way around my shape, carving to my knuckles and eyelids. Stone filled my throat, took a cast of my teeth and stretched along the creases of my palms. I could stay here, I briefly thought. I could mime a bust.

I came out the other side gasping. Matthew was standing there ready to move but I held up a hand, doubling over, and gave him the universal 'I need a moment.'

"Can we get back out this way?" I asked, panting.

"It'll reconstitute in a couple seconds," he said. "But I'll give it another shot on the way out."

We stood in the rear atrium, off to the side where a long hall led to elevators and the front entrance. A camera over the rear doors sat pointing at the empty security desk.

"There's gonna be a guard at the front desk. Might see us on camera when we head up," I said. Matthew nodded and pulled the stunner out of his belt.

"How does it work?" I whispered.

"Headshot," he said. "He'll be out for hours."

"I do not wanna accidentally kill some graveyard shift custodian."

"He'll wake up with a hangover. Promise." I nodded. "Stay here?" I nodded again. Matthew crept forward, hugging the far wall, out of view of the rear entry cam. He snuck forward around a corner and I lost sight of him.

Seconds later he came jogging back around the bend. I looked at him with wide eyes.

"Like a baby," he said, adjusting the mouth of his ski mask. We marched forward as a pair, and slipped into an elevator.

Upstairs the door to Pollard's reception area was locked. Matthew held the tunneler up to it, and with another nasal 'UMP' we stepped through the gentle whorls of mahogany. Different materials carried different sensations it would seem, and I shimmered through the wood pleasantly, tasting sap, bitter varnish, nutty cellulose.

The quiet leaning shadows of the reception held echoes of the bustle from when I was last here. All the furniture seemed askew, maintaining the negative accommodations to a larger group. Diamonds of space.

Wordlessly I walked past the desk to the door to Pollard's office. I could feel something from the other side; as though the specter of that headless, frayed corpse sat crouched, just beyond the threshold.

The door opened to a touch and swung inward. Matthew came up behind me, tunneler at the ready, and we stepped inside.

Within, we could see the cleanup crew had done their job. Some stickers ran up the wall denoting position, but if not for that you'd never know we stood in violence.

Matthew pulled out a flashlight and crept around me, doing a sweep of the room nozzle-first. So he felt something too. Hate-ghosts, parading. Together, without a word, we searched.

I checked beneath the chairs as Matthew rummaged through the desk. He checked the drawers, pulled up the holo-panel (everything confiscated and erased), appraised a conspicuous paperweight. I walked in circles, checking the corners, the cornice, the baseboard, running my hands along the walls. Finally, after spiraling, my eyes came to rest on a grated vent just below the ceiling, its blades angled out. I motioned to Matthew and gestured up to it.

We dragged a chair over and I hopped up. It was close, but I couldn't quite reach. In silence we began a clumsy maneuver wherein Matthew crouched in the chair seat and I lurched atop his shoulders. He rose shakily to his feet, his weight shifting on the diamond button tufting. Fumbling forward, I could feel that the screws to either side of the grating were already loose. While Matthew struggled below me I twirled them out of place and tore the grating from the wall. Matthew tilted, and for a moment I thought we would tumble to the floor, but he found his footing and leaned me forward toward the vent. I lay down the grate at an angle and reached in.

I grasped around, flopping my hand about in search of the smallest idiosyncrasy. Finally on the slick aluminum sheeting of the vent's left wall my fingers brushed across coarse needles of Velcro. I crawled my fingers forward, reaching for any attachment. My heart sank.

I felt nothing.

I shifted my weight forward and leaned farther, Matthew grunting below me. With his head pushed into the wall in front of him I could feel the full patch of Velcro beneath my palm. There was nothing there.

"Let me down," I exhaled, exasperated. Matthew lowered to a crouch and I toppled off behind him. He swiveled around and sat in the chair, looking up at me as I collected myself, adjusting his eye-holes back into place. "There's nothing." I rubbed my eyes through the mask. "There's some Velcro where something was attached, but whatever it was is gone." He looked down at his lap.

"Fuck, Sue."

"Yeah." Matthew shook his head.

"Alright let's get the fuck out of the city. To a safe

house." I felt like crying. "It's not your fault. Let's just go."

I couldn't move. I stood there, stranded.

"Let me back up there, Matthew."

"Sue, come on. Let's go."

"Give me your flashlight. Let me just get a look around."

Matthew sighed. He stood, and handed me the flashlight. He got back into the chair, crouching.

"Come on, let's do this quick."

"Thank you."

I fumbled back up onto his shoulders, feeling quietly manic. I couldn't quite say when the blue had wormed into my brain but it was there, and it guided me back up to the vent. I rode forward on a wave of cyan, and shined the angry white LED into the aluminum hole. In the shimmering reflection I peered deep into the vent, and saw the passage disappear into shadow. Matthew grunted again as I struggled forward, his face bumping against the wall. I shoved my head into the duct.

Everything fell away.

In black there were palm trees. They crawled up out of shadow, fronds of tin at a sway, bowing to the globe of flesh that was the size of the world. A globe of skin in blackness.

In the eddies of flesh was a life. In the open wind that rushed through the black, there was a musk, a warm sex. It tingled down to my cunt and I wept, and was carried to the sky. In goosebumps I saw senators, I was wrapped in ecstasy and a singleness, a security, wherein the horrors of power are dispersed, a vacuum state where hatred is quelled to the dumb din of childhood.

I was wrapped in blankets of the clearest blue flesh. Imagining a woman for the first time, crouched on the floor of my mother's bathroom. The perfume of a candle in the night. The raucous ocean while I fucked on an empty beach. Myra frying eggs in an old apartment. My feet dangling from a high chair as my mother lights a menorah, she talks about her mother and cries.

Enfolded in cerulean, skin leaked into my nose, my mouth, my lungs; I sat cradled in the blue womb and grew weary in gentle rocking.

A ship in flames, a breached scream.

I am in a lobbyists' firm in Ohio.

I am a senator. I am in Roman Pollard's office.

I am a frightened old woman. I am in Roman Pollard's office.

I was washed across the flesh in the sodium and chlorine of evening.

Matthew was shaking me from below, his head wriggling between my legs.

"*Sue*. Christ, *Sue!*" he was urging in a whisper.

I was sprawled out, the upper half of my body in the vent. Matthew was trying to pull me down. My eyes refocused in the blaring light of the LED shrieking off the aluminum. My attention turned to the patch of Velcro beside my head, and in the ragged black there was a knot of fibers, a veil of thread. Like someone's sleeve had brushed up against, just there. It was the vilest green.

"Muller," I said, gasping, as I fell out of the vent. Matthew plopped me down, patting my arms.

"The fuck, are you okay?"

"Muller," I gasped again.

"Who?"

"The fucking secretary. She has the camera."

"You just blacked out with your legs wrapped around my head and it was the secretary?" I nodded, slumping down on the floor.

"We gotta find where she lives, Matthew. We need to get to it first or they'll make it disappear."

79

"What kind of asshole makes a video recording of all their shitty deals anyway?"

"Paranoid Nazis. Come on, help me up, how do we find this lady's address?"

He pulled me to my feet and we marched back to reception. I could tell I wasn't the only one that felt lighter leaving that room. Matthew moved away from me and started looking around, for what exactly I didn't know. At that point we'd just been circling in the dark for too long.

I sat down at Muller's desk and found the recess to bring up her holo-panel. It lit up blue and orange, making ghosts of its surroundings. The desktop was patchwork, a mess, but there was a working hard drive. I suppose after all that, it was still just dumb luck that whatever ITB tech had pulled files here hadn't closed their session. I scrolled through reams of appointments, bullshit. After a while Matthew came by and sat over my shoulder. My eyes were bleary and I had a winding headache. He pointed to the screen as I moved from folder to folder.

"Payroll," he muttered, his hand outstretched.

I stared at a long list of a bad man's employees. I wondered if they were all bad, too. 48 hours ago I had worked for Right River, so who's to say.

We found 'M'; and we found Wendy.

The address was on Long Island, near Hempstead. Matthew wanted to wait until morning, but I urged him on. Through wood and stone we left the Hackney for the last time. We returned to the Acura, both sweaty from our ski masks. I felt delirious. Matthew sat in the car, his hand on the ignition, thinking.

"So, what, we're just gonna break into this woman's house?" I grabbed a water from the backseat and took a long pull.

"Yeah," I said, wiping my mouth with a sleeve.

"Did she kill him?"

"I don't know."

"Why would she kill him?"

"I don't know."

He started the car up, and we pulled out of the city onto the highway.

"What happened to you in the vent, Sue?"

"I dreamed."

"What did you dream?" I stared out the window, into the dark. I could see the East River.

"I'm sorry, Matthew. I don't know." I held my head in my hands. "Maybe I'll know tomorrow." He glanced at me. "Something's not right." I rubbed my temples. "We're up the wrong tree."

"What does that mean?"

"Safety isn't what we think."

"So here we are, driving to B and E an old woman's house on Long Island because of a dream you had." I nodded.

Muller lived at the end of a long row of Tudors on a quiet block of kempt lawns. The Acura crept to a halt curbside by a small two-story with a front of variegated brickwork and a steeply pitched roof.

"Okay, game plan?" Matthew said, turning to me.

"We're gonna walk through a wall, Matthew. And then we are going to kindly, with as little threat of violence as possible, scare this old woman until she tells us where the camera is."

"This is so fucked, man."

"The information you want is in that house." He stared back at me. "I'd stake my life on it." He shook his head and pulled on his ski mask. I did the same.

Together we left the car and approached the house. At the crux of the front gable a soft light shined through a window on the second floor. My heart yammered under my ribs. As we came closer I realized something was off; the front door was ajar. I motioned to Matthew, who was heading for the side of the house pulling the tunneler out of his jacket. I gestured to the door and he doubled back. Together we crept up the porch steps.

Through the cracked door a light shined wanly across wooden floorboards out to the brick portico. I peered in through a sway of dust motes and could make out little. Cautiously, I pushed the door open.

Crossing the threshold we could see the house was a disaster. Piles of old newspapers teetered up to the ceiling, books and stacks of outdated media storage leaned amidst heaps of mail from decades ago. A tangle of ancient telephones sat across from a shrine to Christ piled high with empty lipstick tubes, a small electric candle flickering before a crucifix.

Silently we crossed the foyer and in the oppressive must, floorboards creaking beneath our feet, I became gradually aware of a groaning from somewhere in the house; a long string of vowels tumbling in consternation. Matthew had the tunneler at the ready and I pulled the snub-nose from my overcoat and let it lead the way. The newspapers were shedding, and parts of the floor were covered in a rough confetti. A tabby crept somberly through the mulch, ignoring us, and headed for the kitchen.

Light was filtering down in dust across a staircase that banked up to our left, and as we neared it the moaning grew louder. At the foot of the stairs I looked up, and Matthew with me. The stairs led up to a landing and after that doubled back out of view. Vowels dribbled down from above. I took a deep breath and led the way.

We moved as quietly as we could, but past a point there was no disguising the creak of the stairs beneath us. As we rounded the bend we came upon a white door, leaned open.

With that same streak of blue, I stepped through.

Muller was sprawled out on the floor at the foot of her bed, groaning, a hose of vicious copper pointing up in her hands, swaying through her wild hair. Her eyes lit up as we entered.

"Uuunhhh uh uh," she grunted, "devils in the house!" She looked up at us. "Wild devils!"

"Hi Wendy." I adjusted my mouth-hole, keeping the snub nose pointed in her general direction.

"Careful," Matthew whispered to me. "That thing she's holding will turn your head inside out." Muller moaned, wouldn't stop moaning; she thrashed around, pulling the soiled coverlet about her.

"Oooaahhhh you've come to collect me? Wild devils, from the black lake!"

"Oh no. Wendy, you okay? We can help you if you need help, Wendy." I tried to hold the gun somewhere ambiently between her and the floor, not wanting to set her off but wanting to shoot first if the copper tube started to angle away from her own head. The nozzle stroked her chin, grazed up the side of her face. I pulled my ski mask off, to a disapproving inhale from Matthew. "Do you know who I am, Wendy? Do you need help? No devil here. We can help you if you need help, Wendy."

"Kike bitch," she spat. "Devil kike bitch. He's in *light* now, already told you kike bitch, he is in *light*. They thought they could ruin him, they thought they could tear him down. Now they'll never, now he is cast in gold; he is a luminous light in the White Kingdom."

"Who's trying to tear him down?" I knew that here in hell were the answers. "Where's the camera, Wendy?"

"Oh they knew he was a faggot and they were going to tell the whole fucking world! He *struggled!* He begged every day for God to break him and make him new again! He was a *good man.* And now he'll always be."

"Wendy, who was blackmailing him? That's all we're here for. We can get you help."

"Reeeeeeeeee – " she started blathering.

"Oh Jesus, Wendy, *who?*"

"She's off her fucking rocker, Sue," Matthew murmured behind me.

"Aah – aah – aah – the fucking *Hill* of course!"

"What? What do you mean the Hill? Lefties on the Hill? Are there any lefties still around?"

"Unnghhh," she rocked, "no lefties. His loyal constituents." My head was spinning.

"His... Well Wendy, I've got some good news. If it's the Hill you're after, we've got just the guy, I've brought you a real live Peacer," I said, gesturing to Matthew.

"Great," he flapped his arms, exasperated.

At this she burst into gurgling laughter, and I thought finally we had lost her. She heaved and hemmed, giggling until she doubled over, the copper nozzle scraping arcs across the floorboards.

"A Peacer?" she screamed with delight, holding her sides with glee. "Oh no, darling," spittle leaked out her pursed lips, "oh *no*, darling," her eyes bugged out, wild, "if you've brought a Peacer, well then you've brought a *government man!*"

She went red in the face, slobbering, a reticulation of veins raising up along her throat and through her temples, she went blue, to purple, her tongue a knob of garish meat; she reeled, a cartoon grape seizing on the floor. Thrashing, dejected, she put the copper to her face and I dove for it; but not before her head was a mist upon the moldering sheets.

"The fuck does that mean?" Matthew pulled off his ski mask, brushing a dew of gore from his overcoat. I stood there shaking, staring at Muller's ravaged body.

"What?" I turned to him, in a daze.

"What the fuck does that mean, *government man?*" His

voice quavered. He lit a cigarette, staring at the mess. I turned back to her, and welled up.

"I don't know, Matthew."

"Jesus. Fuck." He started pacing. "So, what, she martyrs her boss against his wishes and then loses her shit?"

"Look at this place. She lost her shit years ago." Matthew sniffed. He was shaking.

"I really don't know what she meant, Sue. I'm not trying to put one over on you."

"I know you're not, Howard." I moved over to him. "You've had every opportunity to make me disappear." I patted his cheek. He took a deep drag, shook his head.

From over his shoulder a hideous green caught my eye; Muller's cardigan, bundled up in the corner of the room. Moving over to it I crouched down and started digging through the pockets. Some wadded up tissues, chapstick, a matchbook, and then – my fingers touched something flat and cool. I scrounged up whatever it was and held it out in my palm. A small DVR cam, one side coated in Velcro.

"Alright," Matthew breathed. "Let's scram."

On the way out the door I grabbed the cat; it was probably wrong, but it felt right. I scooped it up from the kitchen where it meandered around an empty bowl, and jogged for the door.

We hurried out to the Acura, tumbled in and sped off down the silent street while the little thing struggled in my arms. By the time we were out of the neighborhood it had curled up in the backseat.

"Where we going?" I asked, as we pulled back onto the highway.

"Somewhere quiet."

He pulled off the road at Little Bay Park just across the East River from Throgs Neck as the sun was rising. We stopped the car in an empty lot, a veil of trees and jagged rocks between us and the water as the sun came up gray and delirious. I put the camera on the dash and fiddled around with it until it bleeped, then swiped the image up onto the windshield. We sat back while the cat slept.

A green-clad arm pulls the covering away and gropes toward us. We come unhinged, spinning out of control into blackness. Rewind. Pollard sits at his desk sipping a coffee, he smiles and greets Wendy Muller as she enters. She pulls a length of copper tubing out from behind her, Pollard raises his hands, confused. There is a sizzling discharge, Pollard's head tears apart, his chair trundles back into the wall. Rewind. It's early morning. The office is empty. Muller steps in, looking around nervously. She retrieves a length of copper tubing from beneath Pollard's desk, before retreating to reception. Rewind. Pollard is on the phone, angry. Rewind. I walk into the office, Pollard waving toward me. I sit nervously across from him, gesticulating. He grows irritated. "Vultures on all sides," he coos. Rewind. Pollard makes calls from his desk, meets with another television personality, shares lunch with the Idiot. Rewind through days of drudgery. Pollard masturbates at his desk. Rewind. Time-stamp reads four days prior to the announcement. Three men stand in Pollard's office, their faces register distantly. Don Gable, Jonathan Fredericks, Colm Malone. Senators. White, pasty men. Two sit down across from Pollard, one leans over him. Pollard looks confused.

"I don't understand," Pollard says, laughing genially.

"We need you out, Roman," says Gable, across from him.

"We've been working on this for over a year. I'm very confident."

"We need you to pull support. This isn't up for debate." Fredericks, from over his shoulder.

87

"What *is* this?" Roman asks. He becomes somber.

"This is a firm request," says Gable.

"Have you all gone fucking pink on me? What in the world is this about?"

"The world has moved since you were in office, Roman. Don't worry yourself with details, just crush the bill," Fredericks says, leaning in.

"And if I refuse? I have principles, you know. I have supporters to appease. This is outrageous."

"Your supporters think you never remarried out of grief. Let's keep it that way, yes?" Gable says, leaning back.

Pollard becomes downcast, staring at his clasped hands in his lap.

"Leave my office," he says hoarsely.

"You'll call a press conference?" Pollard stares down. He nods.

"Thank you for understanding, Roman," says Malone. Gable and Fredericks move to leave. "Just a moment," says Malone. "I'll catch up with you." The other two exchange a glance before exiting. Pollard sits at his desk, despondent.

"I'm sorry, Roman," says Malone. Pollard slams a fist down.

"Fucking traitors," says Pollard, looking up at him. "Judas cocksucker."

"It's not... listen to me, Roman. The others would be upset with me for saying so, but you should know. It's not what you think."

"Oh please, do enlighten me."

"When you resigned you were too wrapped up in the craze of it all, you didn't see what was happening. It's manufactured, Roman. It's a farce."

"I don't follow."

"The Peacers. We've brought the war economy home." Pollard stares at him, his jaw clenching, unclenching. "It's quite tidy, really. We leak alien weapons to a front of domestic terrorists, then over-outfit the police, the National Guard; we sell weapons to ourselves. The lobbying firms get contracted out, we draft as many competing bills as we like, none of them need pass. We draft a high profile bill like Heaven Forbid, so it seems like we're getting somewhere. We play the insurance groups against each other. If they're in favor on the Hill they get military contracts, if they're out on their ass we string them along with the latest bill. Everybody wins. There's nothing for you to fight, Roman. All is well."

Pollard sits completely still, looks back down at his hands.

"What's your cut?" Pollard asks, looking up. Malone laughs.

"I'll show you what three percent looks like for being a good sport, how's that?"

Matthew sat silently next to me, breathing. At some point the tabby had crept across the center console into my lap, and now crouched there purring.

"Bullshit," croaked Matthew, shaking his head. "No way." I looked over to him. The sun was cresting the waves of the East River, beating down through the frozen image on the windshield.

"Come on," I said. "Let's step outside." I cracked a window for the cat and we stepped out of the car and walked down to the shore where green water lapped at the rocks. When I looked up, part of me could see some aspect of foil clinging to the beech and sycamore.

"People need to see this."

"I know," said Matthew. He lit a cigarette and offered me one, staring out at the water. "I just don't know where to go from here."

The sky swelled, a lurid blue, without blemish.

"Take me to the dreamers."

A Wailing

From the patio there came a wailing. I moved with gummy haste across the house, arms akimbo, and upon my exit found her crouched, desolate beneath the shade of the portico. Around us the raucous fuss of insects, a swelling, ballooned in the heat. Spiny grass crept along the sagging porch. She sat whimpering and I fawned, pantomiming a display of qualifications. It was the year of the snake, and in that way we were both mischievous.

In her way she asked for space, quality, verisimilitude. I, incoherent, inchoate, bellowed only for reassurance, brevity, tact. Please, please, tell me I am good. Tell me I am good and let the worms do the rest.

Upon completion of my charade she dragged me back into the house, I stared all the while back toward the mangled vines, encroaching, and protested through limpness.

That night a meal was prepared of remnants, and we sat distantly across the vast expanse of dining table. I hemmed and guffawed, knocking my bowl about with rough paws, matted in bristles. She hung her head low and sipped broth. She told me, "You are a figment," to which I answered, "You are the handle of some sour thing I have brought upon myself."

•

In bed we lay feverish, and the creaking of the house was a deafening symphony. I curled and batted, whinnied, bunching the covers in a scrawl, scrambling them to serrations. She sat prostrate; immobile and exasperated.

In the small hours, sequestered in a chapel of sweat, a crash thundered through the house from the kitchen, tinkling above the cacophony of splinters. She gripped the sheets beneath her head, squeezing in balled fists, wringing the sweat from an archeology of bedding. With a grunt of fear I sat up, blinking, and tumbled to the floor.

Panting, the anvil strikes of my weakling heart led me across the endless house. For a moment, as I struggled through the den, in the cupped musk I was consumed by the nearest sensation of bliss; staring at the moldering couch I could remember the heat of a growling fuck, a thoughtful hand upon a shoulder, and all was light, but that then passed. I was left blind in the brackish pit. I scurried ahead.

In the tender maze I was an animal, and I crept in increments through the unending dark. Passing from knotted carpet to lacquer, my toes found purchase finally on the spotted tile of a hall lit softly by the dappled apparitions of obstructed moonlight, garbled, vexed through an array of quarreling branches.

The tile meandered on into cabinets, rough furnishings, the dusting of termites, and in the uneven light a cascade of silver glass was blasted across the kitchen floor, fleeing from angry vines clawing at the sill. Reaching fingers of green had closed in, suffocating and eager, they could be seen through the hung sash to girdle us with spilling leaves and gentle tubers.

The vines tumbled through their broken window and lay about the pale sink, heaving with exertion. Approaching,

I could see a dismal slime excreted across the porcelain.

I returned to the room to inform her we were violated.

In the morning, a welter in my belly sent me careening for the toilet. Panting atop the cold seat I could hear her thunderous footfalls as she crashed around the den.

"The kitchen!" I tried to yelp. "By God, forsake the kitchen!" And yet in the grumbling of my bowels I was a mute, and suddenly there was blood, yes, and a terrible stench. Black blood pouring from me, and a shit-stink so foul I gagged, toppling from the bowl.

I puttered around, circling, and in the shit-stink, as it seeped into the house as a breeze streaks through rushes, I could hear the thuds of her long flat feet bludgeoning down the hall, cracking through the maze that led to our feeble door.

Late in the afternoon I found my way back to the foyer. The vines had taken up residence, a system of leaves decorated our loveseat. Pantless and bloodied I made my way onto the porch.

Clawing through tubers I stepped into the grassy field, the rubbery mulch creeping up my ankles, and with a decided pace I fled, walking, yet in flight, from the threshold of our home to the devouring mouths of eucalyptus arching above the portal of rotten jungle beyond.

In the leaves my stench was quelled. The jungle was silent. I walked, and the need for oxygen left me, I walked without breathing into the dark.

Eventually I came upon a wailing. A circle of figures around a sloshing well, water touched by some tremor, spilling out to the jungle floor. A howling figure turned to me.

"What does that say then, the same soul, not reincarnated, but in two living places? An ineffectuality of purpose? The anatomical belies the mystical. The great magical truth is this: nothing shall be revered."

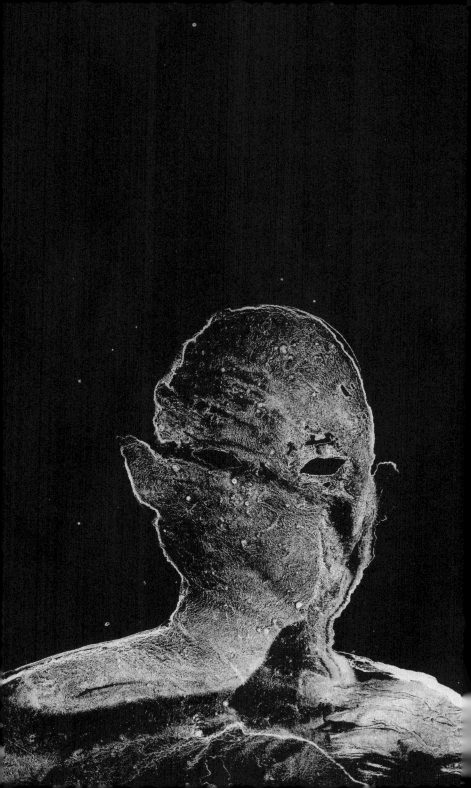

THE LONG MORNING

Our pursuit of the Lunds has proved still fruitless.

In storage containers we have ferried, the drumming rumble of propulsion always a-thrum beneath our butts. In New Zagreb amidst the fuss and ruckus of syndicate squabbles, in the contested zones of contiguous territory I even hijacked us another surveilling craft, sleek and buzzing, to search some colonies out in the deadening rim, but they have continued to elude our greatest efforts.

It has become unclear what is taking place.

It could be that the Lunds are masterful. That was our first consideration and what I thought most likely when we began; that after their emigration, in the years I slept, they had amassed a waxing power – assembled a network of deference and support between stars and crept from view. Yet in scrambling after what little footprints they have left across the colonies, in tracing their jagged path, we came to confront the burgeoning sense that their movements had an inescapable bent of desperation, and paranoia.

Our next assessment was that they had somehow caught wind of our efforts, that they were in fact running from us; a thought that had me giddy. The Lunds! The Danish lords of yore, for so many years my reluctant compatriots, securing their fortress in the soil of the Americas and leaving me scraps to tend; now turning heel before the ugly slave, plucked from beaches of cowries and fresh from his shackles, forever the swarthy pretender posing as lower aristocrat in the darkened soirees of old Portugal.

Fleeing not only from myself, then, but from my compatriot! How they had turned to run before their old thrall, having left her to languish in the hermetic womb of that ransacked citadel.

As I said, we were giddy. What a scrumptious irony!

Yet it is true that this journey, if viewed as a line between two points – from the village of my birth to these gaseous and far-flung heavens – has proved erratic, and evasive of portent, so perhaps a turn such as this was not after all so strange. It is even still true that I may never know what, in all of ghastly space, a lich was doing on Madeira. Is that the stranger turn? The greater mystery?

But while the thought of them cowed continued to elevate me to the wildest heights of fancy, as our hunt drew on, the Lunds' movements proved ultimately too peculiar, and the jolly thought of their terror more complex, for it now seems that perhaps it is not from us they have fled. So what, then, is that dark blade? What hovers, what moves so deftly that they must give their lives to flight?

When the ganglers first presented themselves to the colonies, Biyu and I had been not long about the stars. Their quilled ships descended as great tabernacles from the void. It was a wonder to witness the scraggly sprawl of humanity, forever so eager to condemn, quell their new doubts with such haste. The frontier spirit of the new age was still alive and well it seemed, for better or worse, and the ganglers were looked upon as new allies, the spark of some great opportunity whose barest glimpse was mayhap worthy of reverence. Anyhow, society was only splinters now, empire as enterprise.

While we circled the rim tracking the scent of the

Danes, now and again coursing back to the inner systems, the ganglers captured the glint of human finance. I remember well that gleaming hull sinking above the spires of Novyy Moskva; I was preparing for bed and Biyu sat out smoking on the balcony. It happened just before dawn and she came in shouting my name. We ran back to the veranda and she looked out with awe as I hid behind curtains from the glimmers of sun, peeping into the scalding air to catch a glimpse of its belly as the alloy quills brushed past tower windows, early risers shivering and agog. I remember knowing finally that there were those still less human than I.

What these sleep-muddled petitioners wanted, and want – spilling coffee from their balconies, wide-eyed and gaping – is not control; but rather to be gifted control by a father. They want to venerate, and regard.

Biyu says no, always. No to the rotten ganglers, they are meddlers and swindlers. Biyu is always right.

Biyu says: "I slept a hundred years in a bank!" She says, "What in a whole darling world would I want with a banker!" She says, "My father was a dolt! A boor and a lummox!" She says, "What in a thousand million years would I want with a father!"

Straddling the craggy rim, we spent a long time. There was first the urgency of the hunt; we both had ants in our joints from long sleep and to find ourselves in this new ball of black glass jouncing around in rattling junkers through the brilliant whirl of space dust was such a wonder I cannot express. We were always careful, sticking close, taking watch, touching down on nightside so I needn't fear the burn.

After riding the tether out from Venus into the whirling center we found the adjacent stars teeming with activity. They had really set up camp! Sol system was now a backwater it seemed, we were sailing out strong from the boonies buoyed on solar winds and tracking the beaconed path into the black with glee.

Striding first through Alpha Centauri we touched down on an outlying world and spent some time in the domed Garden City where I found no others of my kind. We awaited transport amidst mangroves wound through with bobbing bridges of swollen wood and I felt, in some way, at home. I spent the days under tree cover, straying from the UV lights affixed to the underside of the habitat.

While I slept in branches, exhausted from Biyu's thirst, Biyu crept out and wandered. She reported back with a dozen sacs of pigs' blood, telling of a bazaar held through a network of tunnels that extended from the border of the plantation. In this way we sustained.

Traveling at night through the Gardens, filled with the hiss of transplanted insects, all having developed reticulated peculiarities in the moist filtered air, we made our way to the alloy shafts at the edge of the dome and I sacrificed a day's sleep to view the sheltered bustle of Railway City that lay at their terminus. The stone paving after decades was still as new under the shield's floodlights and the great monorail that circumnavigated the perimeter gleamed in the iridescence like a Garden bug before fading with a whistle into the hazy distance.

Though the system was underdeveloped, as we would later come to see, the city was alive with the dull hum of administration for agricultural production and transport, and abounded with exotic sundries from the Gardens. As there was much produce preserved and shuttled off from here, in making our way to a metro hub we found it was a simple matter to purchase a seat on an outgoing freighter bound for one of the highly trafficked shipping lanes.

That night beneath the rattling stairs of a monorail boarding pad I drank from a man until he was dead, and robbed him, and in turn let Biyu drink from me. The next

morning we purchased our tickets. It was another three days before we were due to leave and we spent the rest of that time amidst the mangroves, as it was there that the both of us felt more at ease.

Our first evidence of the Lunds came at Teton Spire, an industrial center orbiting the third planet of Sirius. Before the quilled ships at Novyy Moskva, and before the great swindling, but after our time in the Huang Emirates, where we had become embroiled in a conflict. My principles, I believe, had got in the way of things. Biyu lost patience with me for a time, holding no loyalty to bloodsuckers herself. I will say that I was confused by my own loyalty. That sentiment of obligation has perhaps now finally left me.

There was a young man there in the Emirates, or at least younger than I, who had been turned on Venus in the early days of the diaspora by a Russian smuggler who had trafficked one good or another since the first World War. This smuggler's conflict with a rival syndicate had carried over to their new home in the Emirates, and promise of a cure for Biyu's thralldom had kept me by their side and carried us to the massacre at New Zagreb. Biyu, as always, was dubious to the end, and I was the fool.

She had forgiven me by Teton, I think. Her sideways glance to scold again carried a humor in it. And it was there we caught our first glimpse of their footprints.

We were pointed to Teton Spire at last by the reluctant young smuggler after the final death of his sire on New Zagreb. Proving quite forthcoming once our alliance was broken, the boy told us the name Lund was known in the business of bloodfarming.

My kind were abundant on the Spire. A distended needle spanning over a kilometer from end to end, the orbital station is a honeycomb of ducts, shafts and corridors with an underfunded security force stretched thin across its breadth. While its accommodations are no triumph of comfort, it withholds all access to the light of the Sirian sun save for on the viewing decks at certain hours, an amenity prized among bloodsuckers. (These days always awash in the pallid sterility of one fluorescence or another, always striding along some silvery bulkhead, I must say I still pine for the amicable age of gas lamps when one could waltz across a nighttime wen in that agreeable flicker.)

Most of my kind living on Teton were young, immigrating there from star systems more central to colonized space and hoping to find a common refuge. With my nose and Biyu's cajolery we found our first small enclave on the Spire, a haughty group, similarly reluctant to speak of the Danes. I am more suited to brooding, but Biyu, while always suspicious, has a knack for the convivial, for making one feel as a co-conspirator, if not for gaiety itself. It was apparent that their quick tempers masked a desire for comradery, and we were soon ingratiated. They took to Biyu as a weary confederate, and treated me with the deference afforded an elder.

Their game on the Spire depended upon the prison housed at the southern tip of the station. Their enclave, comprised of some twenty individuals (they claimed there were other groups aboard) had landed hold of an old docking port near the station's posterior that they could use at their whim, and they had commandeered a small handful of short-distance two- to three-occupancy transport fliers. Convicts were shipped to the station from the planet below and other worlds in the system, oft times by automated craft; and while the chokey clerks were accountable for prisoners once they had been landed and logged, if they never saw them then they never saw them, given a reasonable stipend. Inter-system conveyances were difficult to predict, but cargoes from the planet below usually launched at perigee, and at

103

each such occasion the bloodsuckers would huddle around an old transistor and wait for their cue, piling then into their clanking transports and hurtling out into the starry mess to nab themselves a fresh one.

They shared blood with me, and I shared mine with Biyu; she showed them her mark — the small stamp of ownership tucked in the cleft of her throat — and they told us their story:

"The Danes came to Teton on a civilian transport bound out from York-Shi probably six years ago, standard. They've given us reasons for leaving that place, but it's a muddle what was true. Not long after their arrival Freja spotted one of us up on sixth level — Alal, who you haven't met — banging on slots past non-resident curfew, and asked Alal if she could give her a hand back to her quarters given the guards were about. Freja's a temptress though as you're likely snuff on, she drew in on Alal and they ended up down here as the rest of us were waking and our whole game dribbled out of us. Freja's a wonderful listener. And Alal just sat there reeling that she hadn't known blood royalty when it kissed her on the mouth.

"We met Oscar that night too.

"As much as we all, or, well, can only speak for myself, as much as I didn't want to trust, it was such a flattery to have kin from Old Earth grant an eye not unkindly to our operation, and I know the others felt the same. And so quicker than you might think the Lunds started orchestrating. And they showed us how we could multiply the convicts we were nicking and how we could be feeding more than just Teton, how we could really be making jits for everyone, not just sustaining up here.

"I don't want to say they were unkind; and most of our sires never passed anything down. Most of us were turned for sport, and the Lunds showed us so many things about ourselves.

"We set the farm up in L-Sec in an old hangar they used to use for waste process, we can show you the place if you care to see; it's still stocked though they're gone now, we still make a decent turnover. They gave us the bleeder enzyme. Oscar said he's the one't developed it centuries ago, I still say that's horseshit, he can be kind but he's a liar. Have you ever seen? It's remarkable, they really gush, they go on and on. One suit feeds the lot of us close to a week.

"Once we'd refitted the hangar and got enough suits linked up, we scorched out the old waste tanks and routed all the blood there. The turbines keep it from stagnating, it's a wonder. And the Lunds helped us, they had a whole trade network set up before coming here, and we started sourcing out blood even to markets in other systems, out in the center. It's prison blood so it's nothing prized but we've got enough that we can make quite a net. They helped us get set up. And by the end of the first year everything was moving.

"They lived with us then, too, here in the docking port. We built them a loft up in the back, welded together some crate sidings and built a cocoon of fire-retardant mesh, so it sparkled like it was royal. They had us keeping to a night schedule out of tradition, and we'd switch off weekly taking shifts at the farm or waiting for the perigee runs to ransack transports.

"About three years ago I was working in the farm running lines from new suits to one of the tank hubs, and Freja came down; there's a raised office for them like for a foreman, she came down and said she needed to speak to me about an issue with one of our runners to the center.

"I finished stringing up the suit and followed her back upstairs. There's big windows that look out and you can see everyone working away and tending the suits, and there's a whole web of blood cables that run to the hubs and flood down into the tanks, so I walked up and was looking out at the whole floor because I wasn't often up there, and Freja asked me to look at her and she said my name several times.

"You remember what it's like when Freja says your name.

"She set her face and became coy and asked how I was, said that we hadn't spoken in some time. She said:

'Annika, Annika. Dear, Annika. How are you? We haven't spoken in some time. You've become a fine worker, really one of our finest; a true specimen. I want to salute you. We have rallied as a beacon of blood in the system, and it really is thanks to the diligence of you and the others. What wonders you have worked! Given enough time and effort, we'll be able to move this operation beyond the Spire. I hope that there is excitement. I hope that you all are excited. Oscar and I are very proud of what we have accomplished in so short a time.

'It was not so very long ago that he and I set out from York-Shi, our prospects having dried up. What a dull and dreary place, for all its activity. We had heard of kin such as yourselves on the Spire from our contacts in the system, and came here looking to start anew. You have all surpassed our wildest hopes, truly; there is a fervor in you that was just waiting to be spurred! Oscar had become such a dour boor before our leaving that place. He has lit up again like a candle! You see, despite our time together, I am still so often at the behest of his temperament.

'How old are you, Annika? How old when you were turned? And how many years now, as kindred? Had you already taken to the stars? Were you abandoned? How long before you found others like yourself?

'Oscar and I have been bonded for many ages; perhaps more than you have imagined. I breathed the air of Old Earth before the Christianizing of Scandinavia. Freja is my true name, but for many years after my baptism I was known as Ella. I reclaimed my name in the 18th century. Oscar, once Agnarr, had grown accustomed to his and has never returned to it. But Agnarr he was, and we were matched and married in the royal court of Gorm the Old in the year 943. Or that is the Christian year, as they name it now. You mustn't mention these things to him; I'm just talking. Oscar is a grouch about remembering.

'I have seen the rise and fall of so many powers by his side as to be beyond counting. And yet despite this eternity, for all that, it has never seemed the less strange. I am still aghast with wonder. I have never felt at home, not once since leaving the shores of Jutland. The Americas were a labyrinth and a knot and a horror. What frivolity youth begets! And this reign into space was for a time almost more than I could bear. Every star and every fire is a terrible eternity.

'I was turned seven years after our marriage by an honored guest to Gorm's court, Margrave Folcher; a visitor from the Duchy of Saxony who had come to talk of trade and of Christ, and who was known for keeping peculiar hours. We held for the margrave a midnight banquet to honor his coming, and again a week hence to honor his departure. I recall him making quite an impression upon my husband. At this latter festivity amidst the ruckus and fuss of the men and their drinks I was pulled into the barn by the margrave, and in the rough hay he spoke to me of the infinite terror of agency, and he gifted me unending will and murdered me and fed me his blood and kissed me until I was full, and he asked only that I spread the dread of Christ and of ceaseless life to my countrymen.

'I was feverish for weeks and lay abed while handmaids tended to me. I told no one of my attacker. It was not until a fortnight had passed that I apprehended I could no longer visit the sun.

'It is an uncanny thing, perceiving one's own desire. I took a handmaid first. I was so hungry I killed her, young and fumbling as I was. The mess frightened the help and Oscar finally agreed to see to me. His dawning was weak and slow, as he can sometimes be, but he loved me still, his young countess, despite my newfound cravings. He would bring me blood from the king's sheep, and as I grew stronger I think he found me formidable, and perhaps more desirable for all that. He began to keep my schedule, telling his staff that the margrave's habits had appealed to him.

'It was still several years hence before he agreed to the sentence the margrave had gifted me. Having never been taught, my attempt was a mess, and the bed was soaked through with my drippings before he awoke. But I remember still as he opened his eyes through the gummy redness that they were filled with tears, and he chortled in the sodden sheets and gripped me to him, groping at me and licking with a darting tongue. I remember that I felt as though the room were filled with the hum of prayer of those before me, of hymns to the great halls where it was said one would live forever.

'Christ was simpler to accept than is often admitted, He was another God to us who had so many. I was baptized at midnight mass at the dawn of the second Christian millennium with Oscar by my side. We felt blessed for the coming of the new age.

'Oscar has perhaps forgotten his good fortune. He has forgotten a great many things. In his defense, it is difficult to remember. There is so much time. A fallen globe, a milky ornament, it hangs and sways and in the silver light I feel that I am no wiser. Oscar has fallen off. Or this is what I fear. I know him as I have never known another. As few have known any, to be sure! I must say that despite our millennia of companionship, time has only served to elucidate our separateness.

'The sorrow of that disunion is a maw to ravage many suns.

'Oscar has become remote. He thinks I do not notice, that the patterns of our interaction have become such superstructures that they have hidden his heart from me. He is naïve. I see his heart, but I cannot guess at his aims. He is perhaps frightened? I am frightened with him! But I do not know of what.

'In all of Yggdrasil and the Godhead of Christ this is not as promised. Not this separation. The Holy Love is catastrophe. I am lashed to the hull of this plummeting craft that is the size of the world. In our shell of secrecy, lined against the bulkhead, he lies there at noon thinking I do not know he lies awake. The pace of his blood has changed. He is changing. Yet we have given up on change! It is a game for the young. We adapt, perhaps. We do not change. And yet there he lies.

'We have moved across the stars, attempting to redirect this.

'Dear Annika, you are still young. In so many ways, you do not understand how young. I am strained. I feel it in the spaces between what makes up the rest of me, in my residue. I feel chewed. My paths of probability dwindle, the blur of my movement becomes more precise as my choices narrow. To feel trapped in this way, now, and here, is such a jest I cannot contain it. My life unending, compounded by this vastness, and I can only sit. As a young woman thinking on the infinite, I thought only of Christ. I now can think of nothing but the abyss.

'Annika. You see, you must help me. Oscar is fading into some new mold. And I am mired, unable to think. Every word he speaks he has spoken to me – so many times before. Each meaning takes no new form. All that he says angles and flattens, takes some reflective reference to a shape of action and inference we furnished at a time so distant that I feel I cannot myself comprehend. Annika. I am in hell! Annika. Please. I will instruct you, and you will do as I instruct.

'You will follow Oscar. You will watch where he goes at night while the rest of us work. You will watch how he moves. You will watch who he speaks to on the station. You will make lists of who he speaks to, and you will watch them also. You will make lists of who they speak to. You will watch where he feeds and when, and in what quantity. You will take note of where he travels, and how frequently. You may be seen, but you must not be seen too often. You may speak with him, but you must not speak with him too often. And you will write all this down. You will provide me updates. You will present me with a web of his movements, you will collate and you will deduce, you will provide me with patterns and theses until you can provide me with the equation that is Oscar. You will do this, and I will reward you. You will do as I say, Annika. You will do as I say.'

"When I left the room I was dizzy, my head was a muddle. I spent the rest of the night fiddling at suit lines. The next night I started following Oscar. What struck me first was that he never seemed this floundering betrayer that Freja had in some ways made him out; he seemed irresolute maybe, or like he was lost, but not in a way like he minded or was frightened. Or no, that's wrong too, he *was* frightened, quite, but not of being lost.

"The first night I followed him he spent mostly wandering the Spire. I trailed behind, sometimes waiting in different corridors, letting him disappear from sight, then catching up to him at the next. He walked almost to the top of Teton. Spent hours watching players at the slots, sat for a while with a group of foundry workers, saying little, smiling at their jokes. As morning came he returned to our hangar and climbed abed, and I did the same. The next several nights were similar. I started keeping a journal, an hourly log of our movements:

1900 – M-Sec Level 4, Oscar spends several hours with smelters in the aft barroom.

2200 – P-Sec Level 2, Oscar speaks to a kiosk vendor on the promenade about their wares, rechargeable stimulant rings from Barnard's Star.

"On the fourth or fifth night he wandered up to a barroom in E-Sec and the barkeep greeted him like she knew him. He lingered around 'til her shift ended, and together they walked up to a viewing deck on the top level, taking the long way. On the way up the barkeep told him about her week. Oscar tilted his head and listened, and she talked of lingering clientele, a friend who had moved down planet-side, a message from her brother on Novyy Moskva.

"On the viewing deck they were unaccompanied. Except for me, of course. I've learned to flatten myself in shadows, in a way that I thin and become less, it's a thing I've taught myself. Several of us can do it. I still don't know if that's why Freja picked me out, or for some other reason. I like to think that she saw some other thing, that's my greatest indulgence; believing that she favored me.

"Up on the viewing deck I flattened and I watched them. Once they sat down the barkeep stopped talking, and from the viewing shields you could see the rising face of the world below, the glimmer of fliers in the distance, the twinkle of another planet far off. Oscar looked out with his lips a little bit apart. Eventually the barkeep looked up at him expectantly, and Oscar started talking. He spoke about a scrap shop on Old Earth and the man there who would take in trucks full of jagged trash, wires to be stripped, silicates harvested from old chips, ancient cathode tubes that he would hang in decoration, and he talked about the man's daughter who would bring friends into the shop at night and they would wrap themselves in cables and ragged mesh and

111

grapple with each other, they would dig through mounds of glittering junk for any display that still flickered, poking and prodding for some response, a bleep or a stutter, or read what text was legible through crumbling glass.

"As Oscar spoke he drew closer to the barkeep and her back straightened, but she was so excited, not scared, it was the strangest thing. And when he clamped down on her throat, the story that stuttered on his muffled lips came bursting out of hers, and she shook as he fed, her eyelids jittering, spouting words about the man's daughter rolling around through the electric trash.

"When he was finished, they separated; and they stood and they *bowed* to each other. She wandered off and I followed Oscar and watched him spend the rest of the night in a mess hall all the way on the other side of the station. He sat in a corner 'til everyone had left and then walked the kilometer back to the hangar and to Freja.

"I told Freja about this early the next night. A little dark thing lit up in her, she was so excited and so sad; she told me 'yes, good, keep watching.'

"A couple nights later a similar thing happened, this time with a foundry worker from C-Sec, greasy from working the machines. Oscar and him took a long walk to the viewing deck at the top of that section and on the way up the man confided in him. He told Oscar about his debt troubles with a syndicate bookie, about a woman from the Com-Labs he'd been seeing, how he'd had a drop-off in correspondence with out-system friends since the solar radiation had picked up that week. When they got up to the deck they sat in silence, waiting for the last few patrons to leave. The two of them leaned back against the bulkhead and looked out at the rising world and Oscar, with less hesitation now, started talking.

"He spoke of a man named Uther, and of Uther's blade, and that the blade came from an icy lake; a hand had snaked up from the lake and given Uther his sword and with it he'd defended the Bretons, but that the sword was maybe not from the lake, it was maybe yanked from an anvil, and if it was then the anvil was not an anvil but a great tree, and Uther then was rather Sigmund, who would sire Sigurd, who would slay the dragon Fafnir, Uther then maybe a lie, or something similar but with more merit.

"He spoke in waves, of legends, and he was either present in them or he uttered the retelling as though he were always present; like a god. Or some figure, a thing in the sky. The words rushed out in waves and in the gurgling runoff my agency was diluted, I felt lost in the eddy.

"And it was the same then, as Oscar spoke he drew close to the man and the man shivered and was eager, and Oscar put his hand on the machinist's chest and went in on him; and as soon as he bit, the man continued on where Oscar had left off, crying out desperately for Fafnir, and Oscar nursed on him until he quieted and mumbled on about Sigurd, later Siegfried, and all the people who wrote of him, and then Uther; poor Uther.

"Oscar had many of these friends, that was how it seemed. They loved him! But still he was frightened of something, and sometimes when he would move towards them, as they shivered I could see him tighten, for a second he'd pause as if something would descend on him. Then that moment would let go and he'd nuzzle in.

"I was enamored with this voyeurism. I spent my nights flat and in the dark, watching. I fed off blood from the tanks. My brothers and sisters would ask after me, and I'd tell them I was honored by the Lunds, doing work for them elsewhere on the station.

"I kept following, and flattening. I would follow Oscar every night for nearly two years.

"I met with Freja often. Sometimes she'd confide in me her troubles, her anxieties, or she'd speak to me as if I were Oscar. She endlessly wanted his feeding time stories.

She didn't know where they came from, she would press me for details, leaning back with her eyes toward the ceiling. Sometimes she'd fall asleep while I spoke; she'd wake up and start rambling some vacant story of her own.

"I stopped questioning, or thinking much about it after a point, I circled into the rhythm of Oscar. It felt to me that I was their child, or something like that, some other drooping part of their marriage. I felt trapped; and I couldn't wait to see more, every night I relished it.

"A little over a year ago, on the M-Sec viewing deck – it has these slatted partitions so the light of the world comes up in bars – Oscar sat down with a woman who worked as a foreman near the tip of the station, she'd been on Teton for decades and she'd come all the way down to M to see Oscar. He had her leaned back into the bulkhead and her face was touching the wall and she kept opening and closing her lips on the metal like a fish; and he leaned in and he told her the story of my life.

"He talked of a young girl on Dàshān Reka at the center, chafed thumbs skimming pads at the surveillance farms, and fleeing then from the Oval Action, the mother hiding at the farm in rows of dangling metal limbs that sway like kelp, and the way the chains of sparks light up her face in a crazy blueness, and the girl moves from the virginal protectorate into the spinning assembly ring, and out in the ring the syndicate arms are so focused on stemming the raiders threading their net that home base is the wild frontier for runners and boomers, and a bloodsucker finds me for a night of fun, and then long nights figuring out what's what and how I eat now, with no one to show me. I was so alone before I came here.

"And he bites the woman and she's murmuring into the metal, 'Annika, Annika in the ring, feeding off orphans in the drainage ducts, what a brute, what a waster, Annika whose mama died in flame, she finds her way to the Spire tasseled and wilting, she is a whole new kind of debris, Annika stirs blood into shit vats; Annika finally meets a friend. Annika is trash, Annika is mineral, Annika is the light and the way. She is the rowdy end. Annika is how the pieces fit together.' In the shadow I flattened into almost nothing.

"I never spoke to Oscar, once I began following him. Freja told me I could, but I never did. I felt that I knew him, even if I didn't know what was happening to him. I lost my head in this vain effort, and I drew away from the ones who took me in, I stumbled through this crooked agenda. To be on Freja's errand was to be blessed, and to share their marriage in this small uncouth way was divine. I was gifted the love of God.

"Not long after this, Freja asked if she could hold onto my journals, said that she wanted to look over them. I go over this transaction again and again. Her hair was teased out, like with static, she maybe smiled but I don't remember, she was brusque. The next night the two of them disappeared. They left no notice. The common claim is that none saw them go. How you could miss the sight of Freja and Oscar Lund walking side by side is beyond me. As I'm being honest with you, I'll say I felt betrayed. They ran from something in the night. Even from the two of you, one could think. And not a word to me! Freja after all that maybe thought I was empty, that I was an urn for Oscar's oddities. I felt more a shim than a cup. But what's a couple of years to them. I taste bile when I think of it."

We stayed that day with the enclave in their hangar. They let Biyu and I sleep in the Lunds' royal cocoon, and all the hours spent in there I was alive with the scent. I raked the sheets while Biyu lay snoring beside me. With every tussle I was covered in particles of them, the Danes coating me like confetti. The litterbugs!

The following night I asked that they show us to the

bloodfarm, that I might inspect their operation, and the Lunds' offices, though Annika insisted they had left little. She took us through a viewing deck on our way to the old waste reclamation facility, and described where Oscar had sat. Oscar Lund is a bastard, but I didn't tell her that.

From our angle hovering over the planet, trails of industry could be seen streaking through the atmosphere. Biyu was enamored with the view. Annika warned of second sunrise at the top of the hour, advised that we follow her back below. Biyu, not fearing the glare, was reluctant.

The bloodfarm whirred. The hanging suits were quietly tended to, the gurgling lines extending into hubs a-hum and rattling and then down into the waste tanks, turbines sloshing through endless gouts of blood. A multitude of suits were sedated along the walls, some murmuring quietly at the ground, heads lolling.

I have never found the practice of farming to be anything but shameful. Profitable, certainly. But full of shame. The more civility comes to bloodsuckers, the more they want their meals out of a bag.

The farmworkers eyed us without a word, some bowing their heads. Annika brought us up the oxidized staircase into the elevated offices, with big plate glass shields looking out to the farm. A desk chair reclined behind an alloy bureau, the drawers jutting out. I rifled. Annika was right, there was very little. Some tablets detailing shipment calculations. A small brick of cargo mite repellent. A can of duster. Freja's scent was everywhere.

I moved to some lockers in the corner, but these too were empty. I found two strands of her hair caught between a nut and a washer at the underside of the second shelf. I left them as they were. Clues, as it happens, are mostly found in people.

•

It was many years later that in despair I suggested we turn to the ganglers for aid. I think it was not long after this that Biyu left. Thralls feed not on humans but rather only on the blood of those they are bound to, and having shared much blood with the Lunds as a young vampire in America, I was able to sustain her for years despite the absence of her patrons; but in our travels we had found a synthetic substitute similar to what the smuggler had promised us in the Emirates, and her will to be unbound had stagnated, as had our search. To be fair, I imagine I am a tiresome companion.

Biyu is impulsive, she can be fiery and she can be cool, but I have never found her tiresome. Her wisdom comes top-down, it is not as logical as it is comprehensive, or like she sees the thing from above, how each hand touches the next. She figured out the ganglers before I did.

She took a lover at Novyy Moskva. I believe she found some transformative notion, or some soft sense of home there, the spires rising like mangled towers of Guangzhou. I can picture her looking out at their high nasal apertures, the landing pads and flaring archways, aware that she can thread their needle, she can traipse between dealmakers, that she has shed all gullibility; but also that in that moment what she feels she wants is love, and to come to know a place, to map a city within herself, and not a galaxy. I have met him only once, the lover. I am suspicious of all lovers, though he seemed bright and thoughtful, if childish. Biyu, in her fiery way, can make any companionship seem a continual vista.

I am unsure to what extent she has made her nature and her condition explicit to him.

I myself have been more restless. I do not know if I continued the search for her sake, as patronizing as that now seems to me, or if I continued because the desire to find the Lunds was in some way mine all along. Perhaps both are accurate. I was reluctant to turn to the ganglers after Biyu's harsh dissent, as it brought me to a place of shame, but after more useless fiddling in the rim it is still where I have turned, to my regret, as I sit here now behind the white shield of their brig, its faint buzzing long past the threshold of maddening.

It has been years since we've spoken, and so before approaching the Hegemony I wrote a letter to Biyu, as best I could, along syndicate lines of transferal. I wrote:

Biyu -

I hope this finds you well. I hope that Novyy Moskva, or wherever you now may be, has proven a continual source of fulfillment to you. All that I wish for you is fulfillment; whatever that means. The line of time can confuse these ideas. I should rather say that I hope your residence is a journey that has not slowed. Biyu! I write to you because I have not written to you. I hope that whatever familial resentment you may carry, it does not impose a dread over your receiving this. It is funny that I care what you think, aha! But I do. I write because though it has been years since we parted, it is you who sits in the lobe of my brain, to whom I pose all questions. Your ethics have wormed into my endless stubbornness. You know what is rotten and you explicate it with the certainty of a child; it has infected me. When I sleep you are next to me. When I journey you prod at the rudder. And Biyu, I could not keep off our trek for long, despite your abandoning it. I must find them, you know that I must.

I write to you because now more than ever, you sit in my mind screaming at me. I turn again to the ganglers, and I cannot help but yelp back to you. The ganglers know the structure, I know no way around it! The structure for everyone else is confused, but it feels to me that the Hegemony has mapped it, so that they may drain it of resources. This trove of info is a feeding trough to them, the brats. I know they are despicable, I know they are sly, I know every argument. But this search has become a farce, and if I am ever to find the Danes I know not where else to turn. I write to you because I am in need of your scolding, I know that I walk into quicksand, I feel reckless and I miss your firmness.

Frankly, for me, our years apart have been disposable. I move out of repetition, I cross an abyss, I work, I mingle, I look back to the abyss. Every syndicate state is a dull bed of the same horror, the grasping desire for some vacant thing that is never in reach. There is never recognition, there is never fulfillment. There is holdings, and probings, and the desire for more. Desire is not love, I cannot see that. I see only the wasteland of desire, the radioactive field we found on Burras, that stinking marsh covered in the film of the fat of the dead.

I write to you, Biyu, because, in selfishness, I wish you to know that I am still abroad. I wish someone to know anything about me, in a way I have never felt, but not just someone, I wish it to be you, Biyu, because you are my eternal sister, you are the song in the morning that I will never see.

All my wishes
- Abrahan

So yes; here now, restricted. If there is any state to which I am accustomed, it is imprisonment.

The postmodern prison infuriates, as there is nothing to smash. The white shield lights up, it is a small space, three walls and the shield. If you touch it, it sends rough ringing through your body, remarkably unpleasant. It may have been a while now, it's unclear, no one speaks to me and I do not speak. At the left wall, stage left relative to the shield, a low metal bank carries a narrow strip of spongy foam to lie on. Above the foam an opaque bag of blood is affixed to the wall with a short hose dangling that I can suckle at like a hamster. A thin line extends from the top of the bag up into the ceiling, and when the bag is drained more blood dribbles down into it with a low murmur.

I was brought here without pretense from a Hegemony embassy on Reka. They nabbed me. Black walls closed in, as of nightmare, and I awoke with the foam and the bag. I imagine they find me curious, for I am a curious thing to find; though I wonder that no one has spoken to me. I have had long flights with no speech, but these new centuries have turned me chatty.

I find that the foam is not foam, but rather a tight sac filled with small marbles of some polymer, near the consistency of sand. With my nail I tear a hole into the corner of the pad and spread out a scattering of the stuff across the floor, and in this way I can draw. I've never had a fine hand for it, but I take to it readily in the cell. I draw out sequences, and jumbles, and great curling shapes. I can blow into the wispy field and erase my work and start over, and if I blow softly enough a layer will sift over the valleys and create a new sheet, with the old designs still faintly discernible; and so over time I can draw compound images, the structures of which only elucidate themselves to me as they appear, sprouting from the end of my index like worms.

It is through this pastime – at first plaintive, then meditative – that, unwitting, the ganglers have presented me with the means to see through their great deception. The matrices I scrawl – initially meaningless in the sense of direct ratio – in their function as markers of time passing accrue a symbolic form for me. And in this, the spatial denotation of the temporal, the demarcation of velocity through structure, I get it, I get what Biyu got many years ago but couldn't articulate. They are swindlers, the ganglers; but I had not, until now, ascertained the scope of their swindling.

I am unsure of the timeline, but after I've drawn 734 images I hear a hissing in the hallway of perhaps a door being drawn into its recess, then a successive hiss of its resealing. Sliding footsteps creak down the metal and a form drifts into place, silhouetted in the white of the shield, long, thin and hunched. From it, issuing, a voice:

"Abrahan Inácio Fonseca de Santiago, honored guest of the Ganglekt Hegemony: we bid you rise."

I pick myself up from the floor, my hands slipping through condensation, and scrub the sand beneath the platform as I stand.

"You are summoned by the will of Praetor Sgkeklakt, you are confined to the course of the Praetor's will." The shield curls back from its frame; it hovers, distends, and wraps itself around me, encasing me in a buzzing egg. I balk at its jiggering, shivering, and slowly acclimate to the hum. "Follow closely Master Fonseca, bound by will."

I drift out of the cell as if tethered, my white cage scraping along the floor as we move down the hall. The door opens for us, and as we move into the adjacent chamber I can feel a shift in the gravity, a lightening, as my cage gains a buoyancy and the praetorian loses his slouch. Unburdened, he comes to his full stature, wriggling his shoulders. The rough folds of his skin open into the new lightness, his many fingers flexing, and he stretches to a height of some three meters, my prison bobbing behind him. We drift through the alloy tubing and I can hear little behind the crackling of the shield.

Travelling through a glossy maze of corridors and partitions, we pass others of his kind striding slowly through the low gravity like moon-walkers, their long legs bowed out before them. We move past a viewing port, and through the milky sheathe I can make out the extension of a great structure, rising into starry black.

Beyond the viewing port the hallway terminates at double doors sunk into the wall, meeting in a row of gleaming knuckles. The praetorian kneels as the doors part with a chittering. Within, two more guards frame the doorway carrying staves of light; sparkling threads peel off and drift away, winking out before they can take form. The three turn their eyes inward to the chamber, to the sloping figure behind the bureau, and say at once:

"Praetor, we grant you Abrahan Inácio Fonseca de Santiago, will-bound, for your discernment."

My cage drifts into the room until I am before the desk,

facing the Praetor's figure, and the three leave the chamber, the doors sealing behind them. My cage dissolves and the jangling of my nerves stutters out. I stand there shivering, trying to inhale.

"Sit."

I sit.

"Master Fonseca, welcome to the flagship of the 13th Regiment of the Ganglekt Hegemony. You are here because I wish it to be so. Place a hand upon your head." I do so. "The head has been covered in reverence before the Hegemony." His elbows flare out. "You may remove your hand. Correct your posture. Sit straight before your Praetor. We may begin." His fingers stretch out across the desk, dilating in series. I sit lightly in my seat, almost hovering. All slavers have their ceremony. "Master Fonseca, on Dàshān Reka you entered the sanctity of our embassy with the intent of discourse. State the topic of your inquiry." My mouth is dry. Stretching my lips:

"I was hoping the Hegemony had acquired information I seek. You have a wide dragnet." I clear my throat. "Its breadth is alluring." The Praetor's nostrils part in exhalation.

"You jest? Or you are being playful. I see. Express the scope of the information you desire." I stare at him, my eyes soupy in the low gravity. I suppose I have, after all, come to talk.

"I am looking for one Freja and one Oscar Lund. That is the content of my will." He adjusts himself at his seat, the folds of his skin wavering. His fingers curl back with a quiver.

"Master Fonseca, the Ganglekt Hegemony greatly prizes information."

"How banal," I smile.

"You are a fount, hence your being here. I am to review the quality of your content for propriety and relevance, after which you shall remain either will-bound to me or, if duly determined, be passed into the will of the Consul of the 13th Regiment. If your information proves constructive to the form of the Hegemony, we will consider an exchange." The desk parts, and the Praetor lowers his form into its recesses, the folds of his skin meeting the contours of the separation. The metal begins to glow as the light of my cage.

"I will refer to you as Abrahan, so you will speak to me as you would a friend. Hello, Abrahan. Tell me of your memories of Earth." Pieces of the ceiling detach and his skin spreads up to meet them.

"I have a great many memories of Earth."

"The Hegemony desires to know of them."

"You desire much." His skin seeps into the crevices, he is spread like a web.

"Abrahan, my friend, the Hegemony collates; we deduce and map so that what is known to some may be known to all. If you neglect to submit data, there is no content to comb, and nothing to examine. There is nothing additive and there is nothing progressive. Progress is pure, friend Abrahan. Talk to me of old Earth that we may add to the structure of the Hegemony, that we may try at perfecting our institution." Buzzing white bands curl up out of my chair, clasping delicately to my wrists and bonding me.

"I have lived a long life, Praetor. I grasp the scope of your desire; I do. You are corrupt; you have wormed your way back to corruption. You have abandoned the perfect structure. Holdings and portfolios, they jest at approximating the innocent formation, as they masquerade as desire fulfillment. Finance is not fulfillment, it is a portrayal of inclination. Portfolios pretend at validating time, in that they pretend at illustrating a bridge from your want to the point of the luminous object, but the object is not really present, only the idea of the means; you distribute credit to suspend desire. And as you change the currency, as you sculpt an economy of data, you have obscured also the form of production, and

123

thus the form of value. You shout from the mountaintop, 'One day you will know all!', and yet every thought, every small history is an infinity of knowing.

"You understand the game, you prod the boundaries of temporal impetus, and yet you forget there is no finite structure that can be mapped, Praetor, no such body exists. You toil at the behest of fools."

From the bands at my wrists a numbness spreads through me, like cocaine plankton turning through my arteries; I slouch in my seat, bouncing.

"You are very wise, friend Abrahan," murmurs the Praetor. "Yes, you think yourself quite sage. You believe you glimpse something of us, or that in your wisdom you may evade the mechanism. You are older still than I, yet your impetuosity rings of adolescence. Yes, dear Abrahan, you are an ancient delinquent, a quaint relic of old chaos, and you fail to discern the order into which, as all, you have nestled. You speak of scope, yet that is precisely what you fail to comprehend. I describe not a romance of exploration; I describe an adjudication that is never-ending." Bloody spit dribbles from my lips, drifting, and Sgkeklakt's skin quivers. "Tell me of Earth, Abrahan." My drooping lips wag, and strain.

"Outside Chicago, in 1933, Praetor, we drove in the snow. In a Ford, a Model B Ford, have you mapped Ford? Where does Ford fit? Oscar was a dolt at the wheel, most always. I was, we, we had been staying together on and off, had reconnected at various points, became close again in the '20's. We would sometimes pair off, but it was most often the three of us. I was madly in love with Freja now, sometimes it was just her and I, which was best, sometimes myself and Oscar, we would get on or not. I've never before or since in equal measure so stimulated a man and disagreed with him. What have you mapped about my kin, Praetor? Do you know how we fuck? Would you like me to show you? Oscar liked every arrangement except where he was exempt.

124

I really was so madly in love with Freja. Oscar was a dolt behind the wheel. He was rash; he'd been rash for a hundred years, ever since industry. We drove into Chicago to meet an old friend and attend a gala, and Oscar brought some surprise antiquity for our hosts, something he kept wrapped in a canvas bag, and he would trust no one else with it nor let it from his sight. And he certainly wouldn't let us drive, aha! So he drove, and the sack sat there next to him in the front passenger, and that leaves myself and Freja together in the back, there was no arrangement Oscar could find that he liked. I clutched to Freja's warmth, it was bitter winter and she was the splendid light, and Oscar eyed us in the rearview, his whites rimmed red and blinking furiously in the snow. Freja, asleep, dreamed, and whispered her dreams to me, dallying at my shoulder, her hair tumbling down. We had lost a tire already on our way from New York, along the Pennsylvania hedges, and so we rode now on the last we had and the spare was rent on the ice as Oscar eyed us.

"We crawled on a hubcap to the tree line at the shoulder and I stayed silent, a bit sullen, while Freja cursed at Oscar saying how we were fucked, we're fucked. Oscar says alright, alright, we'll wait for a kindness, and he laughs. I say, 'don't worry dear Oscar, we've yet to find a fiasco that couldn't be remedied in an eternity, no?'

"'Time is on our side,' Freja says. She bursts into giggles and Oscar sits there looking violent. I crack the door and leave the car, huddled, and trudge through the snow around past the fuming exhaust, melting a wedge in the ice beneath it. The tire's a flabby mess. I look into the car at the heat of the Lunds, fogging up the windows, and decide to stay in the cold. I plant my feet in the snow and stare into the night, waiting for headlights. When they blink alive lurching around the nearest lean in the road I raise my arms like a child and wave into the light. America was very nervous in 1933! Or America is always nervous. It was a number of headlights before any crept to a halt. The car came rumbling up into the embankment, tires crunching in the snow.

"The door undid itself with some difficulty and a man stepped out clacking through the ice in a hemorrhaging leather jacket, the wind blowing him sideways, the tassels of a scarf trailing behind him. The scarf covered most of his face, he had a driving cap pulled down low and mostly I could just see the crinkled white skin around his eyes, but he pulled the scarf down to speak, coughing out clouds of fog as Freja and Oscar stepped from the car. You may think me a sight now, but I was quite something next to two white fellows in the Depressive Midwest, and despite that the man called me 'friend', which, though you use it here now to engender loquacity, is not a sentiment that has ever been greatly afforded me by strangers.

"He said to me, 'Ho there, friend! Caught in the snow?' I nodded, and Freja nodded, flushed.

"'We're down a spare!' I called into the wind.

"'Winter luck!' he says. He looks back to his car, up the road, and back at us. 'Well I can't see's how you'll make recompense, I'm not making my stop anywhere near; but leaving you out here would make me nothing but a bastard!'

"'Lend us the spare,' I say, 'and we can caravan to town. We'll replace it.'

"He says, 'Ah, if it can't be done the world's not over. Stay put, I'll have it in a moment!' He scrambles back to his vehicle and returns wielding a wrench and his spare, I hand him a jack from the trunk and he moves to our devastated flank and sets to work.

"'Thank goodness for you, sir!' shouts Freja, 'Thank goodness for you!' before climbing back into the car. The man, crouched, grunts into the cold, and has me hold out my hand for the lug nuts as he peels them off.

"'What brings you out?' he asks, keeping his eyes on the work.

"'We're to visit with friends,' I say.

"'Miserable night for a visit!'

"'Miserable year!' I laugh. He laughs too, his head in fog.

"'True enough. We'll see what Roosevelt has to say about that, thank the Lord! Any day now.'

"'And yourself?'

"'Myself?'

"'What brings you out in gross weather?'

"'Ah, I'm a man out of work! Not a unique pronouncement, surely. Was tending to a farm, south near Champaign, but with the surplus, and winter... Trying for the city, 'til the spring at least. In March perhaps the Happy Days are Here Again?' He chortles and coughs and wrenches the tire off, lurching back and falling into the snow. I move to help him up and slip in the ice, cracking down on my rump, the lug nuts scattering. We both lay there miserable and laughing for a moment, crunching around in the freezing gravel.

"I come to my knees and help him up onto his, we grab at the spare and hoist it into place, and then both crawl around collecting the strewn lug nuts. The two of us scrabbling around under the car, I say, 'You really needn't be this kind.'

"'In all honesty, I'm not,' he says. 'Was nearly asleep at the wheel. I figured a chat in the cold would get me going again.' I scoop two into my hand, my teeth chattering.

"'If we're being honest, I've no idea what tire shop would be open at this hour; but if we caravan to town we can square you up with a meal, at the least.'

"'An offer I won't refuse,' he says. We struggle out from under the car and start getting the lug nuts back on. From the rear passenger window I see Freja's hand scrub out a spot in the fog, she kisses her fingers and places them on the window, and I reach up and pat the glass. 'What's your name, friend?' he asks.

"'Abe.'

"'Hullo, Abe. Aleister.' We nod to each other, he wrenches the last of the lug nuts back into place, lowers the car back down. 'That should have you,' he says. Oscar's hand goes through the back of his head, and his eyes fall flat, I jerk back into the snow spattered with red. Oscar rears up behind, the blood misting off his arm.

"'Fuck off, Oscar!' I shout. 'What the fuck good was that!' He crunches his hand down farther, through the bone plate, 'til his fingers come out Aleister's eyes, he stretches into the mutilation and works a thumb behind his jaw, puts on a low cartoon voice, working his head like a puppet:

"'Hullo Abe, hullo Abe,' he laughs. 'Hullo Abe, get in the car! Get in the car, Abe!'

"I stood up, sullen, and Oscar flung the body off his hand into the snow, reddening.

"'Get in the car, Abe,' he said. I climbed in next to Freja, and Oscar started up the engine. Freja smacked him on the back of the head.

"'You are an ass!' she shouted. 'A true ass!' We moved off down the highway. 'What a fright for that stupid man.' Oscar settled into the leather.

"'Winter luck,' he says. Freja falls asleep on my shoulder."

I fall silent. The Praetor's web of flesh drifts in the milky luster, splayed. How to go on from here? My body is numb, my tongue lolling out my mouth, my eyes are turned half-blind. I bob about the chair, strapped in by light.

"Praetor, I am not your friend," I slur.

"I am imbued," he replies. "What resplendent facts."

Every prison is this milky hole, every boundary a whiteness. I have forever lived in a freedom of my own wakefulness. What is all of space, but the Atlantic?

"I am refreshed, friend Abrahan."

Where is that beautiful people to whom the extrasolar

is a thing only to be recognized?

"You will divulge to me your million histories!"

From the drawings in the sand I then can see the convergence; how everything is met perfectly, as perfection is the only meeting. I see how the convergence is a recognition of placement; that everything has already been placed, is always placed.

I hear the gleaming knuckles behind my head part with their crackling, and hear the footsteps of a praetorian guard. I turn my head in the milky soup of the buoyant eternal prison, the empire that has never ended, to look at the curving gangler marching through the double doors.

"What is this interruption?" asks the Praetor.

In the movement of the guard there is a tremble, a shivering of space, and behind its white eyes a glimmer, and a residue. In its bowing comes a shudder of force, an arc of brilliant sparks issuing from every cranny in the folds of its flesh, a tumult and a celebration, and in every spark, a hundred million times is Biyu, her shape and her form. The sparks whirl through the chamber, scrambling every glittering surface, shattering my bonds, and coruscating across the bureau to alight on the webbed body of Sgkeklakt, who is frozen mid-croak.

You are the one, Biyu. You are the one! We are just beginning, Biyu! We have just begun.

ACKNOWLEDGEMENTS

Many thanks to Greh for templating, formatting, editing and publishing the stories collected here, and for believing in the writing. Thanks to John for his design acumen in the 11th hour. Endless thanks to Solita, Larry, Sam, Meghan, Johann and Greh for their beautiful artwork and for allowing me to use it here. Thanks to all friends and family who gave thoughts and notes on earlier versions of these stories. And thank you, wherever and whenever you may be in the world, for reading.

LEE LANDEY is an author and musician born and based in Los Angeles, California. This is his first published work.

CHONDRITIC SOUND